LAW OF THE GUN

Bill Dosser watched through the peephole in the door as Clayton approached and then stepped out with his rifle, cocked and ready, cradled in his arm. "Stop right there," he told Clayton. "I don't know you."

"I'm new around here," Clayton said. "I came to give you a message. Your brother's dead."

"Dead? How?"

"He was shot by Tom Clayton. Do you know who Tom Clayton is?"

"I know about him. I'll ask you just once more. Who are you?"

"I'm Tom Clayton."

It took a second for it to register and a split second for Dosser's rifle to come up, but by then it was much too late . . .

NEBRASKA AMBUSH

JACK AINTRY

ZEBRA BOOKS
KENSINGTON PUBLISHING CORP.

ZEBRA BOOKS

are published by

Kensington Publishing Corp.
475 Park Avenue South
New York, NY 10016

First printing: February, 1989

Printed in the United States of America

CHAPTER 1

He liked the feel of the leather, even though it wasn't his own saddle and the horse was a stable nag. The sun was high and there was a stiff wind from the west, but he was sweating and it felt good. He was enjoying the endless space of the plains. He was enjoying the day.

It had been awhile. On the trains from the East, one to Chicago and the other heading off to the northwest, he had amused himself by imagining how surprised the girl would be when she saw him, and now an impatience and a kind of excitement was creeping over him. He reined the horse in and, deliberately, his feelings too. "Easy, easy," he told himself with an amused grin. He was a man, a young man but no boy—except when he grinned, and then he looked about sixteen.

To his left, heading off east from the wagon road, was another road, and according to the directions the livery-stable owner had given him it had to be the road to the ranch where Arden lived. Arden. An odd name for a girl, but he liked it. A few miles ahead along the slightly descending road he could see the green patch of the town on the brown and dust-colored prairie. Again he decided to curb his impatience to see the girl and ride into town first to rent a hotel room, have a shave and a bath and get some clothes washed. He would stick to his plan.

He was a lot closer to the town when he became aware of horses and men on the road. Closer still, he could see they were just standing there, only about a mile from town. The horses were at the side of the road, their reins trailed, and the men were planted in the middle of the road looking his way. A reception committee? Certainly not for him; not a single soul knew he was coming. The law? He had heard that Nebraskans were pretty touchy about people riding into their towns packing guns, but he wasn't packing one; it was in the roll behind his saddle. They were just waiting there, clearly expecting him to pull up. Oh well. He pulled gently on the reins and his horse stopped.

"Hello," he said cheerfully. "Quite an honor being met like this."

They didn't have any sense of humor. In fact, they seemed to resent his. One of the men took hold of a rein at the bit and the other two flanked him, walking up close.

"Where you heading?" the man in front growled.

"Who's asking?" Still cheerful.

"We're the law here," the man snapped.

6

The young man didn't like people who stuck their noses in his business and tried to wreck a fine day, but he tried to keep it light. He laughed in a friendly way and said, "You look more like rustlers." And he knew at once that he should have shown a seriousness befitting the occasion of being stopped by the law at a little town in the middle of nowhere. Joking about the power and authority of some petty officials is hitting them where they live. The man holding the rein took it pretty well and started to say something, but the men flanking him moved close enough to touch his legs and the one on the mounting side of the horse rasped, "Get down."

"Aw, now. What for?" It was a reasonable appeal, offered with a mollifying grin.

The man who had ordered him down put his hand on his gun. The young man stiffened in his saddle, staring at the enraged law. Then the man on his right grabbed him and tried to pull him out of the saddle. The young man's reaction was instantaneous and dangerous. He was the type of tall and rangy individual who seems lazy and ineffectual when he is relaxed, but whose muscles are like spring steel, and he had spent his life working hard on a cattle ranch. As he slid from the saddle on the wrong side of the horse, his left foot shot up and caught the man with the gun smack under his chin, sending him sprawling and hurting. Then he swung a left and smashed the nose of the assailant who was pulling at his belt with one hand and his sleeve with the other. He hit the ground and bounced up crouching and ready to charge the man holding the rein, but he was looking

7

into another six-shooter. A bullet slammed him full in the chest, but he tried to charge anyway. Another bullet hit, and another. As he sank to the ground he looked at the gunman and said, "What for?"

CHAPTER 2

Rocklin spotted him right away, and he was just as Bannister had described him — middle aged, weather-beaten, stocky and powerful. His expensive and durable clothes, light gray Stetson and natural air of a man who knows where he is going and intends to get there identified him as a cattleman, a successful one.

Rocklin watched without seeming to as the man, Hanson Friendly, walked through the huge double doors of the cavernous Chicago station and started down the platform toward the train. He was not aggressive or in any way obnoxious, but as he made his way toward the train people swerved out of their paths just a little to give him more room.

The man was looking around, studying faces. He was in fact looking for Rocklin. But Rocklin was watching someone else who had just pushed through the door and was picking his way through the growing crowd on the platform, a tall slender man dressed in black like a western cardsharp, a tinhorn. This man was hurrying a little and dodging people so

9

as not to lose sight of Friendly, but he wasn't trying to catch up with him; a tail.

Rocklin turned away and pretended to be examining the locomotive. What now? It seemed there were things Bannister had neglected to mention. He turned back, and already the crowd had grown. There was a train on the other side of the platform and the people were sorting themselves out as they decided which one was which. Pretty soon it would be like trying to find someone in Washington Square on Saturday night.

Now the cattleman had slowed down to look around for Rocklin. It would be obvious to his tail that he was expecting to meet someone. Rocklin started pushing his way through the crowd.

Chicago! Getting through Chicago was impossible. There were, how many? A hundred and thirty thousand miles of railroad in the nation? And it seemed that every one of them converged on Chicago, like threads leading to the center of a giant spiderweb. And you couldn't get through the city on a train! Freight could, but people couldn't . . .

He lost sight of the rancher, but he could still see the tall tinhorn, who was looking around is if he had lost him too. Good. Maybe Rocklin would have a chance to warn his contact before he gave the whole game away.

. . . And to get from one train station to another clear across town a man had to climb aboard a miserable horse-drawn Parmalee omnibus and travel through a near riot of a half-million milling people . . .

There he was. No, he was gone again. Damn.

He had had to stop in the city this trip anyway, to see Bannister, but it was . . .

There he was again. Now if he could just get to him. Rocklin pushed his way through, paused for a second directly in front of Friendly and said, "Later."

Suddenly the crowd on the platform was thinning out. The conductor for the first time was yelling "b-o-o-o-a-a-a-rd." Rocklin watched Hanson Friendly get on at one end of a Pullman car and the tinhorn at the other, then he climbed on, found his berth on another Pullman and settle down to watch the train pull out of the station. He thought it was a remarkably smooth departure. The new Westinghouse air brakes and the knuckle coupler that had replaced the man-killing link and pin between the cars made all the difference in the world.

It wasn't until late afternoon that he had a chance to pass a few words to Hanson Friendly. He had checked the Pullman ahead of his three or four times but had always found the tinhorn, whom he was beginning to think of as Blackie, planted firmly in his seat six rows back of Friendly. So when he saw Blackie passing through his own car, apparently stretching his legs, he made his way to the forward car and paused beside the cattleman, who was reading a Breeder's *Gazette*.

"You're being watched," Rocklin said. "Don't look up. We'll meet by accident at dinner. Follow my lead."

Hanson Friendly was sitting alone at a table when

11

Rocklin entered the dining area, and, sure enough, two tables away on the other side of the gently swaying car sat Blackie. If Rocklin sat down opposite the rancher he would be facing Blackie, which suited him fine. Only about half of the tables were occupied and the area was fairly quiet, with subdued voices, the ring of silver on heavy china and the clicking of the wheels on the rails.

"Mind if I join you?"

Friendly looked up, the surprise in his eyes not showing on his face. "It's a public place," he said.

A waiter brought Rocklin a bill of fare, took his order and went away. "You're Hanson Friendly, I believe," Rocklin said, aware that Blackie was watching and hearing him.

Friendly looked up from his plate, again surprised. "Do I know you?"

"Name's Rocklin. It's a real pleasure, Mr. Friendly. I've seen you around the Cattlemen's Association. One of the directors, aren't you? Understand you have quite a spread up in Nebraska. Isn't there a town . . ."

"The town's in Nebraska. My ranch stretches over into the Territory. Dakota. It straddles the line."

"I see. I'm interested in that area, you know."

Friendly eyed Rocklin and then turned back to his food. Presently he said, "What is your business, Mr., uh, Rocklin?"

"Oh, I buy and sell."

"And what are you buying or selling right now?"

"I'm going to be buying beef. Lots of it."

"Then you shouldn't be interested in my neck of

the woods. We've been selling to the same packers for over five years — and getting a good price."

"Listen, Mr. Friendly . . ." Rocklin made it obvious that he was about to launch into a sales pitch, his voice, though not loud, carrying easily to Blackie's table. Friendly again looked surprised, and a little annoyed. Blackie more or less lost interest and settled back to roll a cigarette. ". . . I suppose you've heard talk that Shafter is going to open a plant near St. Paul?"

"Talk, yes."

"It's true. Ground has been broken. A year from now, maybe sooner, the biggest packing plant in the country will be going into operation. And do you know how many head of beef they plan to process the first year? Just while they're winding up to a full operation? Fifty thousand!" The waiter brought Rocklin's food.

"Is that a fact?" Friendly said, showing no particular interest.

"You can bet on it. The first year! I know this isn't generally known, but it soon will be. They're going to have to start buying cattle and sheep and hogs right now." Rocklin picked up his knife and fork. "I'm one of their buyers," he said, and started in on his food.

There was silence for several minutes; the rancher seemed preoccupied. Rocklin was about to go on with his pitch when he spoke up. "Looks like quite a seller's market. That is, if people are ready to eat that much meat."

"They are. No doubt about it. You know the

13

Shafter Company. They're not slipshod; they study their markets."

"Even so. Remember the panic of '73? I do. And it's not all that long ago."

Rocklin was shaking his head. "Maybe. But let me ask you something, Mr. Friendly. How many people do you figure live in Dakota Territory today?"

Friendly grunted. "I get your meaning, all right. I never saw anything like it. Close to half a million, I reckon. Mostly foreigners. And just in the last ten years or so."

"And it's not going to stop. A market? You can bet your bottom dollar. Sure, I know, there'll be ups and downs. But you know as well as I do, Mr. Friendly, that the trend is up. Maybe for the next fifty years or more.

"And then there's the railroad. There's a new one going through Dakota right now, isn't there, heading for Montana and eventually the West Coast? Seattle?"

"Damn foolishness. There's no need for four transcontinental railroads."

"Oh yes. Yes. Don't forget those immigrants. Five hundred thousand of them. And think of this: That railroad is coming out from St. Paul, right from the front door of that packing plant. You see? The more we can reduce shipping costs, the more we can pay you for your cattle."

"You don't say." Friendly was staring at Rocklin. "Just to show that they're not greedy?"

"No, because they'll need the cattle. You said it yourself, a seller's market." Blackie, apparently deciding they would be talking awhile, got up and strolled past them out of the car. "That's the man who is following you," Rocklin told the rancher in a much lower voice.

"Are you sure? What is all this? I was told . . ."

"I know. You were told to meet me, that's all. And, yes, I am sure. I don't know what kind of trouble you're in, Mr. Friendly, but you sure are in *some* kind."

"Why all the hogwash?"

"We should keep our voices down. It wasn't hogwash. Everything I said is true. I am going to visit your part of the country as a cattle buyer for Shafter. Now it doesn't matter whether you believe that right now because the important thing is that Blackie believes it . . ."

"You know him?"

"No. I just call him that. The point is that we can talk now without making him suspicious."

"Why don't we just throw him off the train?"

"Because it would arouse the suspicion of whoever put him onto you. And, by the way, who could that be?"

Friendly started to answer, then he stopped and studied Rocklin's face. Finally he said, "Who would you be? I've heard talk around the Association since I became a director . . ."

"Forget it. The less you know about me the better."

"Do you know a man named Bannister?"

"I said forget it. Or I get off at the next stop. Now, who put Blackie onto you?"

15

"Look, I'm in a very, uh, tricky situation." Rocklin waited. "Do I get what you're saying? You actually are a cattle buyer?"

"For the purpose of this job, yes. I'll be able to move around freely, and any deals I make will be good."

"You won't be able to move around freely."

"That will be my problem. I'll have to visit you and the other ranches, and I understand there are only two other really big ones in the whole area, each of them about half as big as yours. And you have almost two hundred thousand acres. Is that right?"

Friendly didn't looked pleased. "Is there anything more about my business that you understand?"

Rocklin ignored it. "Are the other two ranchers, Heismann and Gerald, in the same trouble. Will they be behind you?"

"Heismann, maybe. Gerald . . . well, he's a state senator and has to look out for himself. Well, it's possible I'll just have to go it alone." Under Rocklin's steady gaze the rancher turned a little defensive. "I told you it was tricky. I haven't mentioned anything to anybody about this yet."

"About what? That you've asked for help?"

"Yes, dammit."

"It's no disgrace," Rocklin said, and the rancher scowled. "What about settlers? Homesteaders?"

"No. It's not that kind of a situation. The country . . . I don't know how much you know about the Great Plains . . ."

"I've crossed them several times, but I haven't been

in the northern part."

"Well, it's drier in the western half, all the way down, and the grass is shorter. The sodbusters came in, all right, and they tried, but it's grazing land, pure and simple. You turn the ground over and a hot wind just comes along and blows it away. Oh, there are still some truck farms, some small pig farms, sheep ranches, dairies to the east where they get more rain, but basically it's still cattle country. In that way we've been lucky."

"Government land?"

"Not much. Not anymore. I bought some of it from the homesteaders and a lot—quite a lot—from a railroad that was about to go bankrupt a few years ago and needed the money. Heismann and Gerald are pretty much in the same position . . . that's not the problem."

"The townspeople, then?"

"They could be a problem."

"Why?" Friendly was silent. "You're going to have to tell me about it sooner or later. We'll have time after I get there, but I need a general idea before I ride in. Otherwise, I'm not riding in."

"Well . . . maybe I . . ." Rocklin let it hang there while the man made up his mind. "I don't see what you can do. I don't see what anyone can do."

"Who put Blackie on your trail?" Rocklin demanded.

"Probably the town marshal," Friendly said.

CHAPTER 3

"It was my own fault," Friendly said. "I brought him in, about five years ago. Not on my own, though. People wanted him. At least they wanted someone. There was a pretty wild bunch hanging around the Teritory at that time, mostly riffraff from the Black Hills gold rush, and they would drift into town and take whatever they wanted. There was even talk . . . well, I don't know if it was true. One of the farm girls turned up missing. Never heard from since.

"Anyway, I brought in a man named Fallon. I should have taken care of it myself; I had the men. So did the other ranchers, although they're a lot farther from town than I am. My house is only about eight miles away. But we were busy. It was roundup and . . . anyway, there was a hue and cry and I brought in Fallon."

"Brought him in from where?"

"He had been around the Territory for a while. Ran a little saloon with a roulette wheel and some poker tables up in Gridley. It was a wild town then, nothing but riffraff. Fallon killed four of them, one with his fists, and they made him sheriff. Then I hired him."

"And now your town is the wild one."

"Well, no. That is, there's no crime. No hell-raising, no robberies, no missing cattle . . . nothing."

Rocklin said, "Hmm."

"There's just the cost," Friendly said. "And it gets higher all the time. And I know that Heismann and Gerald are getting as tired of that as I am. Then people—strangers—come through my . . . through town and they get shaken down. A man I know who has a place over the Wyoming line came through town with a few hundred head looking for that new railroad, and *he* was shaken down.

"Fallon has twenty-five, thirty men riding herd on everything and everybody, watching the roads in and out of town. And they're all deputies! They're the law!" The man was nearly speechless with anger and humiliation.

Rocklin allowed himself a humorless chuckle. "The old robbers' guild," he said.

Friendly stared at him with the beginning of dislike. "What?"

"It's a thousand years old or more. Very common in China a couple of centuries ago, and I wouldn't be surprised if it still happens here and there. A robbers' guild."

"I suppose that helps?"

"The head man was powerful and highly respected in the community, and anyone who had anything at all paid protection money to him and his gang. . . ."

"That's it. That's the way it works," Friendly said.

"And pity the poor free lance who is a stranger in town. He robs someone all too innocently and the next morning his head is decorating one of the village gateposts."

"You've got it. And one day they hang the wrong head on the gatepost, and then what?"

Rocklin looked a question at him. Friendly sighed and nodded to himself. "A few months ago we—Mrs. Friendly and I—took our daughter to New York for a trip—you know, the best hotels, a couple of plays, Tony Pastor's—and somehow she met a boy there. I say a boy, but he was twenty-one, twenty-two maybe. An engineering student. I liked the boy all right; he was a good enough boy. But he should have let us know he was coming." He started to pound the table but thought better of it. With an effort he kept his voice down. "You can guess the rest. Apparently he was going to surprise my girl. Happy as you please, like he was taking a ride in Central Park, he rode toward town. Of course he ran into a couple of Fallon's men, three of them, actually. There was a scuffle—the damn kid was actually carrying a six-shooter, or they claimed he was—and he ended up dead.

"I raised all kinds of hell with Fallon, and of course he got rid of his three gunmen, but as far as he was concerned that was all there was to it. Well, that's not all there is to it as far as I'm concerned, Rocklin. I want them out of there. I want my . . ."

Rocklin finished for him. ". . . your town back."

"You're damn right!"

"And you can't depend on the people who live there."

"How can I? Sure, some of them would like to see a change, some who are getting squeezed. But I have no idea who they are and I can't risk trying to find out." He paused, looking as if his dinner had suddenly gone sour on him. Rocklin's gaze was bland.

"All right, I threw a pretty wide loop at one time. Hell, I owned the town."

"Literally?"

"Yes. The land was mine, the store, the bank. But all that was before statehood. Things changed. There are people now, and people just don't like the top dog."

"I see. A lot of them who have nothing to lose like things the way they are. At least they have a law of sorts."

"Right. But the town is dying on the vine, as plain as the nose on your face."

"It's a knotty problem, all right. But we'll have to talk more about it later. I don't want Blackie to start worrying about us."

"There's one more thing," Friendly said. "I think they may be branching out." Rocklin was patient. "About a month ago a bunch of masked men—masked, mind you—hit the Gridley bank—that's the county seat up in the Territory about thirty miles north of Friendly. They got away clean with about

21

thirty thousand dollars."

"Fine," Rocklin said. The rancher, taken aback, glared at him. "If it was Fallon's men, that was their second bad mistake."

CHAPTER 4

Marshall Jack Fallon was in a sullen temper, "sore as a boil where he sits the saddle," as one of his resentful men put it. And both he and his men were very tired and edgy. They had been out five days, running down the men, four of them, who had robbed the bank in Gridley.

The posse, Fallon and his nine deputies, had caught up with the bank robbers just east of the Badlands and were taking them into Gridley—and Fallon didn't like it. Neither did any of his men. Neither did the bandits. One of the bandits had disliked it so much that he had pulled a gun and started shooting, and now he was heading into town hanging over his saddle. The thing was that the bandits were Fallon's own deputies, and when they had recognized their cohorts in the posse they had given up peaceably. Now one of them was dead; the other three were going to be turned over to a United States marshal in Dakota Territory, where the posse had no business to be. So Fallon was sullen and his men were grumbling.

Fallon was thinking about his boss, and if his men had known how dangerously angry that made him they would have kept quiet. His boss, in a cold rage the like of which Fallon had never seen before, had told him straight out, "If I thought you had anything to do with this I would kill you where you stand. Now find them, get rid of them, and take what money they have left back to that bank."

"I can't do that," he had protested. "Everybody will know—" A quirt slashed across his face. He turned a dusky red and his gun came half out of his holster. The cold eyes ignored the threatening move as if they hadn't seen it. Fallon, who was afraid of nothing, turned and started out of the room.

"Wait." Fallon turned. "Take some of your own cash with you. If you have to, make up the full amount of the bank's loss."

Fallon met the eyes, shaking his head slowly. "But that'll be a dead giveaway."

The eyes didn't waver but they grew momentarily thoughtful. "All right. Don't get rid of the bodies. Take them into Gridley."

"How do I kill them without having my own men turn on me?"

"Think of something. That's what you're paid for. And if you can't handle your men turn in your badge."

"I might as well. I don't have enough men to protect all of Dakota. I'm just the marshal of a town in Nebraska."

"That isn't the point, you fool. If you can't use

24

your head any better than that just do as you are told. Get out."

While his men were grumbling, Fallon was cussing himself. He had made a mistake, no doubt of it. When the four men, who had robbed the bank on their own, slipped back into Friendly in the middle of the night, he should have disarmed them on the spot and hanged them the next morning. Instead he had taken five thousand dollars of the money and told them they had to git and never come back. That had been dumb; he had to admit it. He might have known there would be descriptions of the men and their horses, that there would be rumors, and that the rumors would get back to his boss.

"I ain't goin' along." One of Fallon's riders had stopped and was looking defiant. Fallon pulled up and turned his horse, and the rest of the men stopped to look back and forth at the marshal and his rebellious deputy. "Red here's a friend of mine," the deputy said. "We've rode together near five years. I can't go along, marshal."

Fallon drew his gun and shot the man. It was too sudden. All the men could do for an instant was stare at the deputy as he fell to the ground. Fallon backed his horse off a few feet and faced his men, gun in hand. "Anyone else?" he demanded. Nobody moved. Fallon holstered his gun and leaned on his saddle horn. Some of his men glanced at each other but declined to accept the challenge. The marshal had his full share of nerve.

"Now get this," Fallon said. "You men are paid, and paid plenty, to do what you're told, and you quit when I say you quit. You got that straight?" Some of the men nodded. "All right. Now I'll tell you something, for the first and last time. Friendly is our town for one reason — we stick together. Nobody, and I mean nobody, goes off on his own. When these men robbed that bank, I shoulda hung them the next day . . ."

At that instant the prisoners bolted, throwing wild shots back at the posse. It had been arranged by Marshal Fallon.

About ten miles south of Gridley there was an outcropping of rocks, about an acre of them, that rose right out of the plain, the highest being fifty feet. The strange formation was called Deviltooth. High up, some of the rocks grew out of a common base, like huge molars with roots sticking up, and it had long since been discovered that if a good man with a rifle climbed up that base to the place where the roots started to diverge he would be in a rocky cavity where he could hold off an army circling below.

And Fallon had told the three remaining prisoners that if they made a break at Deviltooth and threw a couple of wild shots to make it look good he would let them get away.

As the men rode away shooting, three or four of the deputies drew and fired back, to no effect. But Marshal Fallon dismounted, pulled his Winchester from its saddle holster and shot all three men before they were two hundred yards away. He took a certain satisfaction in doing it, because his four former deputies, wandering around for ten days in the middle of nowhere, had managed to find enough saloons and poker games and prostitutes to squander five thousand dollars, thus depriving him of his profit from their little caper, since he had to make it up from his own pocket when he returned the loot to the bank.

CHAPTER 5

For the third time Rocklin was jolted away from
his meandering thoughts by Buck, who persisted in
snorting and tossing his head. Rocklin thought again
that it was only the intermittent blasts of hot prairie
wind that were bothering the horse, but he was in the
habit of trusting Buck's warnings; he pulled up.
Except for the gaunt trunks of a couple of distant
cottonwoods, he could see nothing but flat grassland
clear to the horizon in any direction. As he sat
searching the 360-degree landscape slowly and carefully, his thoughts harked back to Hanson Friendly
and his problem.

It was a tangle all right, a lot worse than it had
seemed when he first talked it over with Bannister
and then with Friendly himself. It wasn't just a
bunch of outlaws that held the town of Friendly, it
was the law, and the law had gradually been legiti-
mized by the townspeople themselves. First of all,
when the homesteaders had started flocking in a few
years earlier, they had gotten together with the mer-
chants and incorporated the town, with the guidance

of State Senator Kenworth (Ed) Gerald. Rocklin had elicited this bit of information from Friendly himself, and he thought it was small wonder that the rancher was not quite sure of Gerald.

"But," Rocklin had said, "surely the state puts some kind of limit on the tax rate of an incorporated town."

"That's right," Friendly had said, "but the marshal has gotten some of his men to form what they call the Citizens Protective League, and as a private business. As long as the people are willing to pay — or are scared into paying — there's nothing anyone can do."

Buck tossed his head again. "I'm looking, boy," Rocklin told him, "but I can't see anything but grass and dust." Then he thought of the rider who had passed him earlier in the day. The rider, a young man, weathered, easy in the saddle, had stopped and exchanged a few words with Rocklin but had shown no hankering for company. A cattleman, judging from his clothes, he had been well mounted and well armed — anything but a saddle tramp, or even an everyday working cowpoke. But he had been laconic and not overfriendly; he had just wanted to get on.

Rocklin eyed the distant cottonwood trunks, a sign that there could be a creek bed nearby, a possible ambush in a stretch of earth so flat that a twelve-foot rise could be, and often was, called a hill. But why an ambush?

Buck wasn't settling down; if anything he was getting jumpier, and Rocklin leaned forward and patted him on the side of the neck, thinking back on his detour from Omaha to Lincoln after he and

Friendly had left the train. Friendly had switched to another line that stretched northwest to Gridley, and Rocklin had changed his plan and headed for Nebraska's capital to see Senator Gerald. It was the last he had seen of Friendly's tail. Apparently the tall man in black stuck with the rancher all the way.

Rocklin had decided after thinking it over that what he needed was a letter of introduction from Gerald to the bank at Friendly, and he got one. But had he overlooked something? He hadn't noticed anything out of the way on his trip from Omaha to Lincoln, or in Lincoln, or on the train to Ogallala, or on the old and little-used trail north—and he was in the habit of noticing things. There was only that lone rider. Rocklin hadn't the slightest idea that the man knew or cared who he was. But where was he? The last time Rocklin had seen him . . .

Buck snorted again and tossed his head. At that moment the fickle wind shifted in his direction, and for the first time Rocklin caught the faint but unmistakable smell of burning grass. He stiffened in the saddle and every sense, every nerve came alert. First, where was it? He looked into the whipping wind from the northwest. It was there all right, wispy at first and then all too apparent. Even as he watched he could see the line of the horizon from north to west writhe and fade into dirty white. Second, how far away was it? Not far enough. Third, how fast was it coming? The wind told him that. It was faster than he could ride. Buck skittered, protesting the delayed action.

"All right, fella, all right," Rocklin told him. "I'm

considering." Could he make it to the cottonwoods, and the probable safety of a creek bed? His eye gauged the distance, and as he looked he saw, farther away, a horse and rider hell-bent for the same cottonwoods, and he saw the horse stumble and go down short of its goal.

Now — so soon! — he could see a ragged line of orange flame beneath the growing billows of smoke. Buck was dancing around in a frenzy of impatience. It was time to go or stay. He decided against the cottonwoods as too risky; if he tried for them and didn't make it, he and Buck would be finished; there would be no time to set a backfire. He piled off of Buck, trailed the reins so he would stay put, took off his jacket and tied it around the horse's head, then wet his bandanna from a canteen and cooled its nose, all the time talking to it. Buck was not fooled, but he settled down some.

Rocklin set quickly and smoothly to work pulling clumps of the tough prairie grass from the trail under Buck's feet. It crossed his mind that he was lucky the trail was more in the western half of the Great Plains, where the climate was drier and the grass some shorter than in the eastern. It was tall enough to make a devastating inferno, though, as Rocklin became aware when the sound of the fire came, faintly at first, and then with an ominous muffled roar. It wasn't just the searing wind; the fire created its own storm as it swirled along sucking the oxygen out of the air. Damn! What about a stampede? Why hadn't it occurred to him. Rocklin thought it over as he pulled grass, making a protect-

31

ive circle of bare ground around Buck and himself. He had seen a small herd of buffalo a few hours earlier, some scattered cattle, and a couple of antelope. Not much to worry about. Maybe.

The fire was curving toward the east on one side and the south on another, as if it intended to trap him, and Rocklin realized it was getting very close very fast. Without warning a small herd of cattle, maybe as many as twenty, was almost on top of him. In a split second he considered and abandoned the idea of going for his rifle, the only effective weapon against the wild-eyed beasts; it was in the saddle holster a few yards away and he knew it might as well be in the next county. He drew a double-action .38 from his shoulder holster and emptied it at the charging cattle. As he fired his last shot one of them went down and the rest swerved around him. There were three or four buffalo among them. They would all be dead soon. And so would he if he didn't get the backfire lit.

He wasn't quite prepared for the next onslaught, a frantic tangle of small critters; rabbits and prairie dogs scurrying for holes; prairie chickens; dozens of snakes, mostly garter snakes and black snakes, and, worst of all, grasshoppers. They were huge, the ground was seething with them and they half jumped and half flew into anything. He thought of Buck, who would be trying to stand still but whose reins were only trailing the ground.

He lit the match and set fire to the piles of grass he had placed in a twenty-foot radius around him and Buck. He ran to the side of the screaming and dancing horse, wet his bandanna again and soothed its face and nose under the covering jacket. He tied the bandanna around his own face and pulled his hat down. Then he stood at Buck's head patting and soothing him, and waiting.

Still he wasn't prepared for the fury of the fire. It leaped and roared and howled until it seemed to work itself into a blazing tornado that would sweep the man and the horse along with it. Rocklin gritted his teeth and hung on to Buck, who was trembling violently but standing his ground. He thought his clothes were about to start smoking when suddenly it was all over. The fire was moving away as fast as it had approached, leaving nothing but an endless stretch of smoldering blackness. It was hard to believe; the prairie landscape for miles around had simply vanished.

And there was little water left, and no grass for Buck. There was no way of telling how long the prairie had been burning; days maybe, or even weeks. Rocklin knew there was nothing to do but detour back to the southwest toward an old trail town called Gresham—if it was still there. But first he had to find out whether the rider who had raced the fire to the cottonwoods had won or lost.

Small, tangled clumps of grass hidden close to the ground were still alive with fire and here and there bursting into flame as Rocklin, leading Buck, picked his way toward the creek bed. Now and then he brushed away wisps of burning grass that wanted to fly down his neck. Small smoking animals littered the ground. He saw a large black object bulging up from the devastation that he thought was a rock until he came a little closer and saw that it too was smoking. It was a horse. He angled toward it on the chance there could be a man dead alongside it. Buck didn't like the smell of it so Rocklin told him to stay put and went to investigate. The horse still had its saddle and saddlebags, but there was no rider. A bone was sticking out of a blackened front leg and on closer scrutiny Rocklin saw that the animal had been shot once in the head.

Rocklin didn't have to study it out. In a dash for the creek bed the horse had stepped into a hole and broken its leg. The rider, who Rocklin felt sure was the man who had passed him earlier in the day, had either tumbled headlong or landed on his feet running, depending on how lucky or quick he was. Then the rider, who was in a desperate race for his life, took time to come back and shoot the horse so it wouldn't burn alive. An estimable man. Rocklin was squatting and looking at the saddlebags, wondering if there was anything salvageable in them, when he saw the scorched outline of a brand high on the horse's rump. It was a Flying C, from one of the biggest spreads in Texas, owned by a family named Clayton. He searched the ground on his way to the creek bed, looking for another, smaller, black hump. There wasn't one. Maybe the man had made it.

It was Rocklin's habit, and his job, to wonder about things, and as he approached the cottonwoods he wondered why the man didn't show himself if he was still alive and unhurt. He was well aware that any man stranded without horse or water in the

middle of such vast desolation was in bad trouble—
and he had a horse and a little water. But it was also
his habit to size up men. He walked straight into the
dry creek bed and looked around—after reloading
his gun.

The man who had passed him on the trail was
leaning with his back braced against one of the trees,
which had come through the fire with little damage,
and was tying a bloody bandanna wrapped around
his lower left arm. He merely glanced at Rocklin as
though he had been expecting him and continued his
one-handed effort with the bandage.

"Let me," Rocklin said. He untied the bandanna
so he could see the wound. It was long and ragged
and deep, but it bled freely. "Not too bad," Rocklin
said. "I have a kit. I can sew it up."

The man nodded. "It'll be all right in a couple of
days. Thing is, it bled a lot before I realized I had
it."

"Yeah," Rocklin said. He had noticed a small pool
of blood soaking into the ground at the side of the
tree. "I have a little water. And it wouldn't hurt to
carve a steak or two off your horse. Come to think
of it, I shot a steer back down the road."

"I could use either one."

When Rocklin had finished his doctoring he said,
"I'll bring the saddlebags in, at least what's left of
them."

"I'll go along," the man said.

Rocklin shrugged. "You ought to take it easy until
you get some food in you."

The man nodded. "There's some gold, but probably not much else worth saving," he said.

"There's a town about a half day's ride southwest of here. My horse will get us there."

"I'll be much obliged."

"Name's Rocklin, by the way."

"Clayton." The two men nodded, and their mutual trust was sealed. It was as simple as that. They had read something in each other's faces, and it had a bearing on what happened next.

Rocklin had just started for the steaks and the saddlebags and Clayton had turned to sit down next to the tree when they heard a gun being cocked.

When Rocklin whirled, the gun from his shoulder holster was already in his hand. He pointed it at the sound of the cocked hammer, glimpsed the head and shoulders of a man crouched behind a rock with a gun aimed dead at him, and shot twice. He felt the instant tug of a bullet on the left sleeve of his jacket and heard another shot, the boom of a .44 off to his right. The man behind the rock spun halfway around and hit the ground hard. Rocklin slid his .38 slowly into its holster, and only then did he look at Clayton. Clayton was holstering his big Colt and staring at the man they had just killed. He turned to Rocklin. "I didn't have the slightest idea he was there," he said.

Rocklin nodded. "His horse is probably somewhere out there dead. When he spotted me he thought he had a free ride out of here." Only for the most fleeting of instants—and only because of his well-honed instinct for self-preservation—had Rocklin thought of swinging his gun toward Clayton after he had shot the bushwhacker; and Clayton hadn't thought of it at all.

That was why, as they rode toward the old trail town, Rocklin decided to feel Clayton out about his business, that and the fact that on the trail north Clayton couldn't have been going anywhere but the little town of Friendly, or at least through it.

The two men hadn't said much during the first hour on the trail; both were occupied with their own thoughts. They were thinking about the man they had killed—and there was plenty to think about. First, he had tried to kill them instead of joining them, even though three men had a chance of making it to safety if they took turns walking. That said something about the man. Also, there were two small holes in his jacket, obviously where he had once worn a badge. His clothes and boots were old and sloppy, although he carried almost five hundred dollars in greenbacks in a money belt. He carried two guns, one on his hip and another in a shoulder holster, and the initials HPY were burned on his hip holster. His hands were not the hands of a worker.

A onetime lawman with lots of money who would rather kill two men than join them in getting out of a tight spot. And he had probably been riding south—neither Rocklin nor Clayton had seen the slightest sign of him on the trail north—and from where else but Friendly?

Rocklin broke the silence. "Heading for Friendly?" he asked.

"Yes," Clayton said. It was an acknowledgment that they were not talking as strangers but as friends.

"I have some business there," Rocklin said. "Hope

to get a good start on buying fifty thousand head of cattle."

"Fifty thousand?"

"For the new Shafter plant near St. Paul. I thought I might as well start as close to the plant as I can get."

"I've met Friendly a time or two," Clayton said. "Kansas City, Chicago. And of course I know who Gerald is. Heismann's ranch is up in that general area too, isn't it?"

"Yeah. A lot handier than Texas." Rocklin paused and then said, "I've been by your place once or twice."

"You a rancher?"

"Used to be. Full time," Rocklin said. Then he startled himself by adding, "I own a place in New Mexico now, but I live in New York most of the time." Never before had he volunteered such personal information so soon after meeting a man, especially when he was on a job. "Do you know anything about Friendly?" he asked. "I mean the town, not the man."

"Only that my kid brother was shot to death there. I intend to find out who did it and why."

"It's a strange situation," Rocklin said. "You shouldn't ride in there blind." Then he told Clayton what he knew about the town of Friendly.

CHAPTER 6

Arden Friendly approached the spot slowly, leading her favorite bay gelding. She was careful not to make any sudden move that might attract the attention of the sentry on the town's water tower, about a half-mile away. She thought she was fairly safe because it was getting dark and the wind had kicked up a dusty haze. Besides, it was her territory; she had known every foot of it since she was a child. Even in the blackest night she could find the slight hollow in the flat terrain and the slight rise just beyond it where she intended to wait for Marshal Jack Fallon.

She had been thinking about it for days; it had possessed her mind until she had decided just how and when to do it. Fallon had men posted on the road through town, two about a mile south and two the same distance to the north, and there was the sentry on the water tower. It was not easy to do anything in the vicinity of Friendly without being spotted.

The wind that had provided the haze was not so helpful in another way, though; she could never hope to hit any target that wasn't pretty close. She told herself as she pulled her horse down on its side in the little hollow and crawled to the top of the rise that she didn't really want to kill the marshal, she just wanted him to know there was someone around who knew what he was—she had known that from the first, when she caught him looking at her in an insulting way—and could kill him at any time. She was going to make him pay for the murder of Ellis Clayton.

It wasn't because she had been in love with Clayton; she had decided that. She had met him at a riding stable in Central Park when she had been in New York with her parents and he had been such fun, like someone from home. Also he had been at a university in New York for three years and knew the city pretty well. It had been an exciting time. Then Fallon's bandits had shot him dead; and she hadn't even known he was coming to see her.

It was darker when Fallon rode up to make his usual evening check, but the sentries were only about two hundred yards away and Arden could easily make him out. Her shot plowed through the back of his saddle and creased his right hip.

For a second, Fallon didn't realize what had happened, then he shouted, "Get down," piled off his horse and hit the dirt.

For a while there was just the sound of the wind, then one of his deputies asked, "What happened?"

Fallon was white with rage. "Someone took a shot at me," he gritted. He felt his hip and saw the blood on his hand. "Hit me too."

"I didn't hear no shot," the deputy said.

"Came from upwind," the other deputy guessed.

"Upwind. Upwind," Fallon snarled. "Where is that in this damn place. You men circle around a few times. I'm going in and get this patched up. If you see anybody at all, kill him."

The deputies glanced at each other. One of them said, "Couldn't it have just been a stray from somewhere?"

"Kill him," Fallon shouted.

Arden lay very still as the deputies circled around her. They didn't come very near and didn't seem to be looking too hard, as if they knew it was hopeless in the growing darkness.

"What's the matter with you," Hanson Friendly demanded. "What if you had killed him?"

"I wasn't going to kill him," a sulky Arden retorted. "Just show him that . . . well, somebody's got to do something about him and his . . . his dirty pack of murderers. At least he knows now that he's not going to get away with it."

"What he knows now is that he's got to be hunkered down and watching. You've just made things more difficult. And I *am* doing something, but it'll take time. Now you stay out of it."

"Listen to your father, girl," Alice Friendly said. "What can you be thinking, going out and shooting at people?"

"He killed Ellis Clayton, who was my friend." She looked at her father. "I remember a time when you

41

would have killed him."

"You remember no such thing," Alice Friendly said. "Do you think your father just went around killing people?"

"He almost killed that man Fallon sent out to check on the tallyman during roundup."

"That was different," Friendly said. "He tried to pull a gun on me after I had given him a chance to walk off under his own power. Besides, it was an insult to every cattleman in the area. We've trusted that tallyman for years . . ."

"You don't know what you're talking about, girl," Alice said. "Your father came very close to being prosecuted for what he did."

"Prosecuted? For ordering a thief off his place?"

"That wasn't the way some other people saw it," Friendly told her. "And especially that lying sheet they call a newspaper. I was the greedy land baron and that thief was the official representative of the little people. Now this argument is over. You'll never do anything like that again, and that's that. You're lucky you're not in jail right now."

Arden Friendly stood up. She was rigid with anger and embarrassment and her color was high. "And you would let me stay there," she said, and marched out of the room.

"Of course he was shooting at me. I know damn well he was shooting at me," Fallon realized he was almost shouting, but he didn't care. It was as though he was trying to startle some feeling out of those damnable eyes, something besides a kind of comprehensive contempt for all things stupidly human.

"He probably was," the boss said. "And that should indicate something to you."

"What do you mean? What are you talking about?"

Fallon didn't actually see any change of expression, but somehow the eyes seemed to register a deeper contempt. "Have you been shot at before on this job?"

"Never. You know I haven't."

"So something has changed."

Fallon thought this over. "It's just Hanson Friendly, that's all. His attitude has been the same for a long time."

"Possibly. On the other hand . . . I suggest you go away for a few days. Go to Kansas City and . . . do whatever it is you do when you are enjoying yourself."

The marshal stared at the unblinking eyes. "What's on your mind?" he grated. "Say it right out for once."

"You've made mistakes. I wouldn't want you to become a liability. Go away for a while."

He got up abruptly. "I'll think it over," he said, and tramped from the room.

CHAPTER 7

The three men on horseback were astride the narrow trail leading north into the town of Friendly and were clearly waiting for Rocklin and Tom Clayton to approach, making it plain that they would have to stop and talk. Rocklin and Clayton had spotted them a couple of miles back and had seen the town's water tower and the tops of trees on the horizon a lot farther back than that.

The road was as straight as a compass line as it approached Friendly, but beyond the town it began to dip out of sight here and there. It was hard to tell about the rest of the surrounding terrain because of the grass, but the town itself was as flat as a tabletop, making it almost impossible for a man to approach without being seen.

Buck tipped his ears forward and tossed his head slightly, and Clayton's mount, acquired at Gresham, which had escaped the fire, signaled that it too was trail wise. Both men pulled back slightly and their horses slowed to a leisurely walk. No hurry.

They were about half a mile from the three men when Rocklin saw a rider appear suddenly, as though rising out of the billowing prairie grass about two hundred yards behind the sentries and to the east. Clayton had seen the rider too. It was apparent that the rider had topped a small rise and had stopped to watch the men blocking the trail and the two men approaching. He seemed to be slumped or sitting crooked in his saddle, unless . . .

"It's a girl," Clayton said.

Rocklin nodded. "Sidesaddle."

The girl didn't move as the two men continued their casual approach to the roadblock. "She's no great friend of anyone in our welcoming party," Clayton observed.

"Wouldn't seem so," Rocklin replied.

One of the sentries must have heard or felt the presence of the watcher because he suddenly turned and looked at her. He said something to his cohorts, whirled his mount, and started toward her at a run. A second man hesitated an instant, then followed. The girl turned her horse and it leaped into a run, but it was a small horse and the two men closed on her rapidly.

Clayton nudged his horse into a canter, but Rocklin said, "Easy now. Remember, they're probably the local law." Clayton, never a man to hesitate when something needed doing, eased back and tried to sit more relaxed in the saddle, but his expression was as black and hard as obsidian.

The girl was fighting the two men who had closed in on her, but one of them twisted a riding crop from

45

her hand and the other lifted her from the saddle and carried her kicking and squirming back to his post on the trail. The second man was laughing as he followed.

As Rocklin and Clayton rode up to the group they heard the girl saying again and again through her teeth, "Put me down, you dirty killers."

"She's pretty sure the one who shot at us," the man holding the girl blurted. He was a strange-looking man, almost as broad as he was tall, built close to the ground and solid muscle clear up to his bullet head. He looked as though nothing smaller than a locomotive could put him flat on his back.

"Tell me something I don't know," said the man who had stayed on the trail. He was tall and slender, sported two six-shooters, and wore black.

For a second Rocklin wondered if he would have to kill the man he had been calling Blackie, then he realized it wouldn't matter if the man recognized him. He was just a cattle buyer who happened to run into Hanson Friendly on the train. It was always best, Rocklin knew, to keep things as simple as possible.

"What do you want to do, take her into town?" It was the man holding the girl who asked.

"You're damn right. Why not?"

"I don't know," the other lawman said. "Hanson Friendly's daughter . . ."

"She shot at you, didn't she?" the tall man asked.

"Looks like it, but . . ."

"But what?"

"Well, who saw her?"

"What difference does that make? Aw, hell." He turned his horse toward Rocklin and Clayton, who were just riding up. "You two. Stop right where you are. Take off your gunbelts and hand them to Jackson there. I said stop right there!"

The girl, her color very high and her unusual golden brown hair flying about her face, was kicking viciously and repeating, "Let me go!"

Rocklin and Clayton kept coming, almost crowding in on the group. Clayton had controlled himself and his expression had relaxed; it was almost curious. Rocklin, at his most innocent, pulled up almost next to the man holding the girl. Clayton held the eye of the man with two guns and said, "Tell him to let the girl go."

Everything seemed to stop. For a moment there was no movement, not even breathing. The deputies who had been trying to cope with the girl took their first good look at the two men confronting them. What they saw made them want to take a closer look at the situation. The girl was staring too, as her captor let her slide slowly to the ground.

"This ain't your business," the tall man rasped, suddenly hoarser. "We're the law."

"I doubt that," Clayton said. "You don't act like it. I didn't like the look on that saddle tramp's face when he was holding that girl. And Jackson there thought it was funny. Where I come from men like that are asking to be killed."

The tall man turned dark red. He drew. It was all very fast and very simple. Clayton's bullet tore the gun from the man's hand, ploughed in just above his wrist and came out at his elbow. Rocklin palmed the revolver from his shoulder holster and was ready for the bullet-headed deputy when he dropped the girl and went for his gun. As soon as the girl felt the ground under her feet she took off running for her horse. Rocklin rose in his stirrups and hit the deputy just below his left ear and he dropped to the ground as if he had been poleaxed. Then Rocklin turned his attention to Jackson, who was sitting with his gun half drawn thinking it over. It had been a gamble. Rocklin had gone for the bullet-headed man first because Jackson had shown his cautious side when he argued about what to do with Hanson Friendly's daughter. Now, Rocklin just shook his head at the man and reached over and took his gun. It was over. Only one shot had been fired.

"You'll never get into town alive," the tall man said to Clayton.

"Neither will you if you don't get that bleeding stopped."

Rocklin said to Jackson, "Put your pal on his horse."

"There's a man on the water tower," the tall man said, "and the shot was heard. They'll be heading this way anytime."

"And you'll tell them to hold off until we get to town, or you'll be dead," Clayton said.

"So will you."

"Sure. All five of us. Maybe you'd better talk it over with somebody before you decide that's the way it's going to be."

"Don't be a fool, Ranker," the cautious man said.

48

"Can't you see? These men ain't just anybody."

"Shut your mouth!" Ranker, the tall man Rocklin had called Blackie, turned to Rocklin and said, "What d'you think you're doing." Rocklin had dismounted and was gathering guns and dumping the bullets on the ground.

"You don't want your men to see you disarmed, do you?" Rocklin said. "It wouldn't look good."

"They're coming fast," Clayton said. "Four of them."

Rocklin, in no hurry, relieved Ranker of his other gun and shook the bullets out. Then he went around to each of the men, including the one stretched across his saddle, and shoved the guns into their holsters. "Now," he said, "isn't that more seemly?"

The four riders charged in with a cloud of dust. Then they sat and stared. Finally one of them said, "What's going on?"

"Nothing," Ranker growled. "Just a little mix-up. What did you come running out here for? Git back to town and tell Fallon everything's all right."

The four deputies looked around at the group again. Rocklin and Clayton were sitting easy in their saddles, relaxed as could be. "You been shot," the lead deputy said. "And what happened to Gasser?"

"He was talking when he shoulda been listening," Ranker said. "Now git!"

Marshal Fallon, the four men who had ridden in to report, and two other deputies were standing in front of the marshal's office as Rocklin and the others approached. Rocklin was studying the town carefully, weighing the chances of getting out of the

49

mess, not with just his cattle-buyer role unchallenged but with a whole skin. It was a pretty little town, clean and neat. There was actually the beginning of a square, although completed on only three sides. Trees had been planted around the square and in front of each building. The streets around the square were graveled and there were boardwalks on three sides. On the side where the marshal's office was there was a Grange Hall, the marshal's office and jail, and a rambling structure that stretched along the rest of the block and housed a three-story hotel with a dining room, a saloon, and a general store. Fronting the north side of the square was a bank, City Hall, a firehouse, and a freight company. On the south side were a church and three comfortable-looking clapboard houses. The unfinished east side looked out on a corral, the water tower, and the endless prairie. In the block before the square on the trail coming in Rocklin had seen a smithy, a photographer's studio, a newspaper, and a fairly large school. The youngsters, clearly ranging from kindergarten to high school age, were at recess when Rocklin and the others rode by—with one man holding a bleeding arm and another across his saddle—and they were wild with curiosity. One good thing, Rocklin thought; the more curiosity the better. As the strange group drew up in front of Fallon's office, people were coming out of their places of business; a crowd was gathering. An audience. Good.

Fallon, scowling at Ranker, said, "What's going on?" He nodded toward Clayton. "Why is that man wearing a gun?"

"I'll tell you what's going on," Rocklin put in. "We saw these three men manhandling a girl. It looked to us like they were trying to kidnap her. What kind of law do you have in this town?"

Fallon turned his eyes slowly on Rocklin, and Rocklin could see the danger. The man just might pull a gun and shoot. It was on his face, plain to see. It was his way of doing things.

"Are you the law in this town?" Rocklin demanded. It was the right thing to say.

"Who are you?"

"My name is Rocklin. I'm a cattle buyer, and I have a letter of credit to the bank here and a letter of introduction to the bank *and* the mayor from Senator Ed Gerald. Now what about these men who manhandled that girl?"

Fallon turned back to Ranker. "What girl?" he growled.

Ranker swallowed. "Listen, if I don't get to the doc pretty soon . . ."

"What girl?"

"It was Arden Friendly, Marshal," Jackson volunteered. "She was watching us from that little rise back of the roadblock."

"It was her who shot at us the other day," Ranker blurted.

"Nobody saw who shot at us," Fallon said. "I was there, you damn fool."

"Who else could it be?"

"Shut up. Get over to the doc's. Wait. Who shot you?"

"I did," Tom Clayton said. All eyes turned to him.

51

"He didn't want to let the girl go, and he drew on me."

"Who are you?"

"Tom Clayton." Fallon tensed and put his hand on his gun. "I'm here to find the man," he paused and looked around at the deputies, "or men, who gunned down my brother." The words dropped like a stick of dynamite with the fuse burning. The crowd moved back and there were muttered exclamations of surprise. But Fallon was tough as well as dangerous.

"The law is handling that. You from Texas?"

"From Texas," Clayton said.

Jackson was staring at Clayton, examining him up and down. "There's a Flying C brand on his holster," he told Fallon.

Now everyone was watching the marshal. "Well, Clayton, you may own half of Texas, but you're in my town now and you're in trouble with the law."

The unconscious deputy stirred in his saddle. He groaned, and attention shifted to him. "What happened to him?" Fallon asked. Clayton shrugged, and Fallon turned to Jackson. "Well?"

Jackson pointed at Rocklin. "That man hit him." Attention shifted again.

Fallon was sneering. "I don't believe it. Gasser Mann has never been knocked down, much less out. What happened, cattle buyer?"

"The man was off balance," Rocklin said. "He had been holding the girl under his arm and she had just kicked loose and there was a gunshot right then. He was trying to turn two ways at once and draw at the same time, and when I pushed at him he went off his

52

horse backward and hit his head on a rock."

Something about the yarn amused the crowd and there was some derisive snickering. It was too much for Fallon. The blood was rising in his neck and his jaw was clamped. Suddenly he drew.

"You're both under arrest for assaulting officers of the law," he rasped. "Drop that gunbelt, Clayton." Clayton rested his hand casually on his gun. Nobody else moved. "Get his gun," Fallon told his deputies, and two of them, after a slight hesitation, drew their guns and took a step toward Clayton. Clayton's hand tightened on his gun and for three seconds everything stopped dead-still. Then Rocklin spoke into the silence.

"If there's going to be shooting," he suggested mildly, "shouldn't all these folks have a chance to take cover."

"Now that's sensible," someone said. Rocklin turned and saw a small woman, slightly bent with age, crippling forward on one leg and a crutch. "Come on, Marshal, these men don't look like criminals." She looked around at the townspeople with an odd, lopsided grin. "In fact, they look fairly prosperous. Why don't you let them spend some money while you're looking into this thing." There was some laughter, and one man said, "Yeah. Why not."

"I'm Mildred Stocker," the crippled woman said to Clayton and Rocklin. "And I'd be pleased to welcome you to my hotel, the best rooms I've got."

Jack Fallon looked around at the assembled townspeople and slowly lowered his gun to his holster. Then he looked at Clayton. Clayton, who

53

hadn't taken his eyes off the marshal, holstered his gun.

Rocklin dismounted and turned to meet a man who had pushed through to him.

"I'm Brandon Willis," the man said. "The mayor's out of town just now, but I'm a councilman and I own the bank. I just got here, but someone said you have a letter of credit."

"Glad to meet you," Rocklin said. "Give me a chance to get the trail dust off and I'll see you in about an hour, all right?"

"Fine, fine."

Mildred Stocker said, "I'll take you to my hotel." She called across to Clayton, "You too, Mr. Clayton." She turned to a shuffling old man who had been hanging around the edge of the crowd and called, "Newton, take care of their horses."

Brandon Willis called out to Fallon, "These men will be over to talk to you later this afternoon, Marshal."

"Not to me," Fallon said for all to hear. He took off his badge and threw it at Willis. "I'm not marshal anymore."

Fallon sat relaxed, half sneering at his boss with a look that said plainly, "Now what are you going to do?"

Sometimes, his boss thought, he's too easy to read. "That was smart," the boss said. "Very smart." Fallon started to say, "What was smart?" but decided to keep quiet and think it over.

"You'll still run things, of course, especially the business, but you'll have to pick your front man carefully." Fallon was catching up, but he still wasn't saying anything; he was too angry, knowing he was bested again.

"I've quit," he said in a nasty tone.

"Of course. And you were right. It will be better this way for a while. But you'll need someone special, someone with some schooling who will take orders, and who is bright, but not bright enough to get ideas of his own."

Fallon was still plenty mad, but he didn't let it show in his voice. "And he'll be marshal?"

"Of course. Wasn't that your idea?" Fallon, completely outsmarted, sat and glared at his boss. "What about Jackson?" the boss asked.

"What about him?"

The voice sharpened and the eyes looked meaner and colder. "Would he do? He manages to look halfway civilized, unlike most of your gang; he seems to think once in a while and he can be cautious. Is he a coward?"

"No. He wasn't much more than a kid when he rode with . . . No, he's no coward. But what's wrong with Ranker? He's been one of my . . ."

"Ranker's a complete fool. We could have had the state's attorney down on us just like that. Not to mention half of Texas. Now the whole town knows who that boy was."

"It was bound to come out anyway, unless we killed his brother too."

"That isn't the point. Clayton is no fool. Now he

knows just how his brother was killed, thanks to Ranker. Get rid of him."

"Wait a minute. He's helped me keep a handle on this whole thing. I can't just fire him."

"I didn't say fire him. I said get rid of him. I want your men, once and for all, to get the message. I want Ranker found out in the prairie, across the line in the Territory, hog-tied and shot in the back of the head." Fallon started to stand. "Sit down. We're not finished."

Fallon sat down. "Someday," he said, "I'm going to kill you."

The cold eyes didn't even acknowledge that Fallon had spoken. "Will Jackson do?"

"He'll take orders."

"Good. Let's hope he stays cautious."

"What about Gasser Mann? Want me to kill him too?"

The sarcasm was ignored. "No. He hasn't the brains of a cockroach, but his bullying has a deterrent effect on would-be troublemakers. Which reminds me. What about this Rocklin?"

"What about him?"

The thin lips tightened with impatience. "Did he actually swing on that dimwit?"

"Jackson claims he did. It happened too fast. What difference does it make? It was an accident."

"I want to know more about him. Find out."

"He's just a cattle buyer."

"He's very cool for a cattle buyer."

"He could have been the man on the train. I asked Ranker about that just now. He said the man on the train looked more like a whiskey drummer than a cattle buyer, but he did talk to Friendly about a new packing plant. There was nothing suspicious about it."

"Everything is suspicious. Friendly is angry enough to tear this town apart, and he's not going to give up. I know him. And Ranker is sure he didn't do anything out of the ordinary in Chicago? Drop into a Pinkerton office, for example?"

"He's sure."

"Why did you pick Ranker for the job, anyway? He's not exactly inconspicuous; he swaggers."

"He was the only one of my men who I was sure had never been seen by Friendly. Besides, he claims he used to work for the Pinkerton outfit. He's a useful man."

"He has no judgment. Get rid of him. Maybe Jackson will be a little better."

Fallon got to his feet, and there was more than a touch of malice in his voice when he said, "You overlooked one thing."

"What?"

"Some people are going to think Hanson Friendly killed Ranker—and he's going to get the other two men who roughed up his daughter."

"No one who knows Friendly will think that. Besides, as long as your men know you killed Ranker, and why, I don't care what people think. Find out about Rocklin."

CHAPTER 8

Tom Clayton had just finished washing up and was changing to a fresh shirt when there was a knock on the door of his hotel room. He finished buttoning his shirt, strapped on his gun, stood slightly to the left facing the door and swung it open. Arden Friendly was standing there. Her remarkable hair was windblown and she was slightly flushed, whether with embarrassment or anger or both, Clayton couldn't tell. Her hat, a woman's Stetson, was hanging down her back, held by a braided thong around her throat. Clayton decided she was not a great beauty, but she had a pretty little face and her vitality, the excitement of her presence, made her uncommonly attractive.

"I want to thank you for what you did." She said it rapidly, as though she hadn't decided beforehand what she was going to say and had just thought of it.

"You're welcome."

"Aren't you going to ask me in?"

He hesitated. The room was in a mess. Also, what

she was doing would be seen by most folks as improper. He shrugged slightly and waved her into the room.

She took three steps and stopped. "I saw how you made Tom Fallon back down. I was in the square . . ."

"I didn't do that, exactly."

"You refused to give up your gun. What's more, you got away with it. You're the one man who can kill Jack Fallon. Or destroy him, drive him and his gang clear out of the state."

"Why?"

"Why? He killed your brother. At least he was responsible. And your brother was my friend."

He grinned at her. "Sorry, Miss Friendly, I have my own plans."

"I'll pay you."

He felt a surge of anger, decided it was a waste, and suppressed it. But he let a feeling of exasperation show plainly.

She saw it and tried to make amends in an unusually direct way. "That was an insult, wasn't it?" It sounded like a question a child might ask.

He looked at her more closely; apparently she wasn't putting it on. "At least you recognize one when you come out with it."

"My folks sent me to an expensive Eastern school to learn manners."

"And you flunked out?"

She astonished him again by almost laughing. "Not exactly. I just decided that the people back home had better manners, at least more believable."

"I see. Well, I'm sorry, Miss Friendly, but I have to refuse your offer. Now don't you think you had better get out of here?"

She turned and closed the door. "What are you going to do about Jack Fallon?"

He went and opened the door. "You should have studied harder. Don't you care what people say? A small town like this . . ."

"Why should I? People say what they want to if they don't like you. They even make things up. What good would it do me to care?"

"But you do, or you wouldn't have figured that out at such an early age."

"I'm twenty-one." He laughed at her and she turned a pretty pink. "Are you going to help me or not."

"Did you send the letter about my brother?"

"I know nothing about a letter. I didn't even know he was a Texas Clayton. He didn't talk about himself. Are you going to help me?"

"No. What is this crazy desire for revenge?"

"The men who killed Ellis have to pay, don't they?"

"Yes, they do. But do you want them to pay because my brother is dead or because he was coming to see you and you take his killing as a personal insult?"

She swung a hard slap at his face, but he caught her arm and held it, twisting it a little. He stood for a long minute studying her face, feeling the tension and the excitement between them. They were close and it was strong. She didn't flinch. She stared back at him and gradually the angry twist on her lips smoothed out.

He said, "You're a lot prettier, Miss Friendly, when you don't look like a spoiled child who isn't getting her way." He released her arm.

She didn't back up at once, but continued to search his eyes. She favored him with a strange little smile. It was meant to infuriate him, and it did. She turned and left the room.

CHAPTER 9

Tom Clayton's voice was hard with controlled anger. "I want the men who killed my brother. Tell me who they are and I'll be out of your town."

"Now look, Clayton, you're not giving the orders around here," Jackson said. "Besides, you're still in hot water for resisting arrest and interfering with the law."

"Oh come on now, Jackson," Rocklin said amiably, "you were there. You even showed some sense by trying to intervene . . ."

Brandon Willis interrupted smoothly. "Exactly. You know Ranker was a fool, letting Gasser manhandle that girl and then drawing on two peaceable travelers who tried to stop it. Ranker's lucky to be alive."

"What's *the law* doing about the murder of my brother?" Clayton demanded.

"These men are lucky Ranker's alive," Jackson said, "or they'd be in real trouble." He glared at the banker, not for the first time during the conversation, and told him, "And this is the business of the marshal's office, Mr. Willis."

"It's city business and I'm a city councilman," Willis snapped, "and you are only *acting* marshal."

"And *you* are making it hard for me to do my job."

Clayton's fist hit the table with a crash. "I didn't come a thousand miles to listen to your quarrels. What about the killers of my brother."

Rocklin was sitting quietly, seemingly almost uninterested, but his eyes were thoughtful and alert. It was in fact a strange place for an official interview. He and Clayton had been on their way to the marshal's office when they were intercepted by Willis and invited for a bite to eat in the saloon. There was an entrance to the saloon from the hotel lobby as well as from the street, and as they entered, Rocklin had glanced at the light and spacious dining room that flanked the other side of the lobby. Willis had caught the glance and had said, "It's a little quieter and more private in here. Usually no one here but the bartender this time of day and he'll bring us some food and drink and leave us alone." Then he had called to Newton, the old man who hung around the hotel and did odd jobs, to go and tell the new acting marshal where they were.

The new marshal had not liked the setup, or being summoned, or the presence of Willis. He had walked over to the big round table in a remote corner of the saloon—a poker table at night—and had said, "What is this? I do business in my office." Willis had smiled thinly and said, "The ex-marshal did business here all the time." Which seemed to have settled it.

"Killers?" Jackson said to Clayton. "Who told you there were more than one?"

"What difference does that make? I was told. There were three of them and you know it. They killed my brother, not much more than a boy, and they were simply told to make themselves scarce. Now who are they?"

Ex-Marshal Fallon came into the saloon from the street door, took a seat a short distance away, ordered a bottle, and listened to the wrangle. And that, Rocklin thought, is the reason we're sitting here.

"Your brother drew on them," Jackson said, but he sounded less than certain.

"He did not," Clayton snapped.

Jackson turned a dusky red. "Are you calling me a liar?"

"You weren't there, were you?" Clayton demanded.

"No."

"Then how could I be calling you a liar? All I know is that my brother didn't wear a gun unless he was hunting or we were moving a trail herd. He was no showoff."

"Well, like you said, I wasn't there. And I don't know what happened to the men. All I heard was talk."

"Maybe former Marshal Fallon would be willing to help," Rocklin suggested mildly.

Jackson glared at him. "Who asked you? You'd better stick to your own business."

"Then I'm in the clear?" Rocklin asked. He started to get up. "Good."

"I didn't say that. Sit down!"

Willis said impatiently, "What about it, Jackson," and the acting marshal went over to the ex-marshal's table and talked to him in a low voice. Fallon came and sat down at the poker table.

"So now you think you can stick your nose in the law's business," he sneered at Clayton.

"Some law," Clayton said.

"You're not the law," Willis told Fallon. "All this man wants is some information. He's a citizen of the United States and his brother was killed in this town. If you're looking for trouble he's the man who can make it."

Fallon gave Willis a venomous glance and told Clayton, "One of them is dead. Knifed in an alley in Gridley. Dusty Kitt."

"What?"

"That's what he called himself. Dusty. I don't know about the other two. Happy Yates and Bill Dosser."

"What did they look like?" Clayton asked.

"Yates was a big man, almost as tall as you. Sloppy. Hat had five years of sweat around the band. Always looked like he hadn't shaved for four or five days."

Rocklin had an idea. "Did he pack an old .45 hogleg and another gun in a shoulder holster?"

Fallon eyed him. "Jackson asked you before and you didn't answer. What's it to you?"

"Just trying to help," Rocklin said. "We saw a man . . ."

"Why 'Happy'?" Clayton asked.

65

Fallon looked disgusted. "Because he was always so mean and grouchy. Where'd you see him?"

"About three days' south of here," Clayton replied. "He'd lost his horse in a grass fire and so had I. Rocklin came along and offered me a ride and . . . uh, Happy tried to bushwhack us. Oh, and his initials were on his holster. HPY. Sure, Happy."

Fallon said, "And that takes care of him." He was gazing at Clayton with a speculative glint.

"Right."

Fallon's gaze shifted to Rocklin. "You were riding together?"

"Why?" Clayton asked with a none-of-your-business crispness.

"Only after the fire," Rocklin volunteered. "I was farther down the trail before that." All eyes turned to him.

"So you're planning to buy a lot of beef," Willis said.

"As much as I can. You've heard about Shafter's new plant at St. Paul?"

"Some."

"I work for Shafter, under contract." He looked at Jackson. "John Shafter. His office is in Kansas City, Marshal, if you want to make inquiries."

"Appreciate it," Jackson said. "Thanks."

"What's the third man like. Dosser." Clayton asked Fallon.

"Yeah. Well, that's not so easy. He's a kind of everyday sort of guy. Ex-cowpoke. Brown hair, brown eyes, average height and build . . ."

"No scars, broken nose, anything like that?"

"Took a bullet in the hip once," Jackson volunteered. "Limps a little when it's bothering him, like when it's raining."

Fallon's jaw muscles bulged. "That was Happy," he snarled at Jackson, who looked surprised.

"Oh. Was it?"

"So they killed a boy," Clayton said to Fallon, "and you were the one who told them to get themselves lost." Fallon rose from his chair, ready to make it an issue.

"Are we charged with anything?" Rocklin asked Jackson. Silence. Jackson looked as if he was listening for some kind of advice. Fallon kept staring at Clayton and was pointedly quiet.

"No," Jackson said finally.

"Thank you, Marshal," Rocklin said, and he and Clayton rose to leave.

"Better stay out of the Territory, Clayton," Fallon said. "There's no law up there against carrying a gun."

Clayton smiled insultingly. "I'll look forward to seeing you, Fallon. I think you're the one who's really responsible for my brother's murder."

"You're going to go looking for Dosser?" Rocklin asked as the two men strolled toward the water tower and out of earshot.

"Yes. And I think he's around here."

"From the way Fallon acted that's probably a good bet."

"Maybe still working for Fallon. Hiding out up in

the Territory, spying for Fallon on whoever goes back and forth between here and Gridley?"

"Could be," Rocklin said.

"Do you think Fallon's still the ramrod?"

"Jackson sure acted that way. When Fallon was sitting in back of him at that other table he could hardly keep himself from looking over his shoulder every time he opened his mouth. A tough spot to be in."

"Yeah. Fallon couldn't possibly be running the whole thing, could he?"

"Not a chance," Rocklin said. "He's too hot-headed, and he's not smart enough. Let's go back. I don't want everybody to get it set in their minds that we're working together."

"But the head honcho is in town. I mean he's not one of the ranchers."

"It looks that way, I agree. Decisions are made too fast. Like the choice of acting marshal."

"Willis?"

"Could be. He doesn't have the look of a fool about him. But the only way he could handle Fallon would be to have something on him, safely stashed away. A hanging offense, something like that. By the way, how did you get word that your brother was dead?"

"A letter. Unsigned."

"That's interesting. And you said you know Hanson Friendly?"

"Met him a couple of times in Chicago. Just a nodding acquaintance. My guess is that it wouldn't even occur to him to send an unsigned letter. Besides, why would he?"

Rocklin nodded. "So he doesn't even know the boy was your brother. Did the girl know?"

Clayton glanced at him without surprise. "You don't miss much, do you? She says she didn't. And all Ellis told me . . ."

"Your brother's name?"

"Yeah. All he told me in his last letter was that he would be a couple of weeks late getting home from college and he was going to see a girl out in Nebraska."

"Hmm. Well, I'm going to ride out to Friendly's place tomorrow to see if we can do some business. I'll ask about it if you want me to."

"No thanks. I'll be riding out that way myself pretty soon."

CHAPTER 10

The wind was rattling the hotel windows when Rocklin rolled out before dawn the next morning, and it put him in a somber mood, although it wasn't like him to give in to moods or even be especially aware of them. Buck was out of sorts too when Rocklin fetched him from the livery stable and saddled him, but Rocklin knew they would both feel better when they were out in the open heading somewhere.

He was out of pipe tobacco and decided to stop by the general store. It was just beginning to get light outside and the store seemed deserted and dark. Rocklin stood for a minute looking around the place. It was huge and seemed to stretch clear back to the street behind the hotel, where the dim morning light was coming through open double doors. Old man Newton was struggling to roll a steel drum — kerosene, Rocklin thought — through the doors, and Rocklin moved to give him a hand.

"Mr. Rocklin. G'morning." Mildred Stocker had emerged from a small office and seemed to be moving smoothly and swiftly toward him in the lifting gloom. It was just an instant's illusion, but it heightened Rocklin's wonder when he realized how easily she moved about in a tall wood-and-wicker wheelchair and how deftly she put the chair just where she wanted it. Across the handles of the chair was a shelf with pencils and a pen, writing material, order blanks, and lots of cash, apparently money for the start of the day's business. Her lap and legs — leg — were covered with a dark quilt. She was clearly ready to tackle anything, and Rocklin thought she must own the whole complex — store, hotel, restaurant, and saloon.

"Morning, ma'am. I thought I could use some pipe tobacco. Going to cover a lot of territory in the next few days."

She nodded. "You'll find some good stock around here. I don't have much call for pipe tobacco. Prince Albert be all right?"

"Fine. It'll keep me company when I'm settled down for a spell out of the wind."

"From the looks of the western sky it's not going to get any better this day." She smiled, and Rocklin wondered if she was often in a lot of pain. The smile was only on one side of her mouth and she seemed to be gritting her teeth and scowling at the same time.

Newton had finished maneuvering the drum into place and had gone through the front door. He was sweeping the walk, his back to Rocklin, when Rocklin started to mount. A voice said softly but distinctly, "Gasser is after you." Rocklin didn't pause or look around. He climbed aboard Buck and headed north out of town, but he glanced back casually to wave a thanks. Mildred Stocker was standing just outside the store door watching him and the old man was sweeping farther down the walk.

The wind, gusting from all directions at once, was making it hard for Buck to settle down, so Rocklin warmed him up with an easy trot for a while and then let him stretch out in a full run. It settled them both down, despite the wind, and Rocklin tamped and lit a pipe.

He was facing a nasty job, and he didn't know just how he was going to do it. But he was a careful sort of man who didn't rush into things. Usually, when he was sent to sort out impossible messes, he studied the situation thoroughly, decided where the pressure points were, and applied pressure. And it was usually essential for him to walk more or less unnoticed among desperate and dangerous men who would shoot him in the back if they had any inkling of what he was up to. And then there were men from his past, riders of the outlaw trail, who would hear things here and there and in time put two and two together. It was simply a matter of getting used to the idea that at any moment he could become a walking target. Tom Clayton could be a complication. Or, as a distraction for the town and for Fallon's bunch, he could be a great help.

Rocklin thought he heard a faint whinny and he saw Buck's ears swivel, but the wind made it impossible to read the sound, whatever it was. Rocklin had branched off onto the trail heading northeast to Friendly's place, the Circle H, and was about half-way there when he picked out through the swirling dust a landmark that Willis had told him about — Three Rocks. That's just what they were, three big rocks about ten feet high clustered in a triangular pattern. They disappeared in a storm of dust and then reappeared, hardly a hundred yards ahead.

Buck tossed his head and spoke softly to Rocklin. Instantly, Rocklin slid from the saddle and led Buck off the trail, looking around for the highest grass he could find. He discovered that the flat prairie had, on closer look, quite a few handy ups and downs.

It took him an hour to circle wide and approach the rocks from the other side. He found Gasser Mann sitting on the ground behind one of the rocks and smoking a cigarette. He walked up in back of him and said, "Looking for me?"

Gasser swung around, and he had a gun in his hand. But so did Rocklin, and Rocklin's .38 was a double-action Colt. Gasser's six-shooter wasn't even cocked. He stood and faced Rocklin. "What did you hit me with?" he asked.

Rocklin had never seen anyone like the man. He was straight up and down with no fat, just bulging muscle, like a carnival strong man, a sideshow freak. "My gun," he said.

"Get rid of your gun and hit me again."

"Don't be silly," Rocklin said with a grin. Gasser holstered his gun and started for Rocklin. "Hold it." Rocklin pointed his Colt at the man's chest. "Stop right there." Gasser kept coming and belted Rocklin along the side of his head with a roundhouse right. Rocklin was stunned, literally and figuratively. He didn't actually want to shoot the man; it would bring all kinds of questions and complications. He would have to keep out of his way until his head cleared and he could decide what to do.

Gasser was no skilled fighter; all he had was brute strength, a low center of gravity, and endless faith in his own invincibility.

Which, Rocklin thought, might be enough if he wasn't careful. He circled, staying out of Gasser's way. When the man swung and missed, putting himself in just the right off-balance position, Rocklin put him face down on the ground hard enough to knock the wind out of him, bent his legs behind, locked them together at the ankles, and sat on them. He took a firm hammerlock and waited. Gasser soon realized that the more he struggled the more it hurt, and he lay still. His mouth was half buried in the dirt, but that didn't stop the stream of colorful names that sputtered forth.

"I'm ready to talk when you are," Rocklin said, and waited until the man stopped cursing. "Who sent you?"

"Nobody. You knocked me out!"

"Now I believe that's a true answer. How about this? Who actually runs the operation in town, I mean the top man?"

Gasser was silent for a full minute while the rusty cogs went around in his head. "Who the hell are you?"

"Wrong answer," Rocklin said, bearing down.

Gasser grunted and said hoarsely, "I don't know. If you ask me, nobody knows. Only Fallon. Let up!"

"Is Dosser still around?"

"Oh. You're with Clayton after all. Ahh! All right, all right. I don't know. He probably is. He was one of Fallon's pets."

"Good enough. Now I'm going to explain the situation to you. I'm guessing that somebody, at least one other person, knew you were going to ride out, take a short cut or something and lay for me here. Okay, this is how it is. You never met me. You missed me in the dust storm or I went some other way or something. Think it over.

"I'll be riding back into town in two or three days, and anyone will be able to see that nobody has laid a finger on me. Understand? So if you claim you did jump me and somebody wants to know what happened, what are you going to tell them? Are you getting the idea? Nod if you are. Good.

"Now if it gets around that you did see me, then it will also get around that you and I had a little talk. That's all, just a little talk. So you just might end up dead, right? *Right?* Good. I could probably save myself a lot of trouble if I killed you right now.

"It's up to you. I'm going to let you up. You might consider the wisdom of getting on your horse and not stopping until you get to New Mexico or California or somewhere. Don't get up right away. Take it easy and give your bones a chance to settle back into place."

Rocklin got off Gasser and whistled for Buck. But

the bullethead surprised him again; he rolled up from the ground, put his head down, and charged. Rocklin's reaction was pure reflex. He palmed his gun and chopped. The butt of the Colt with Rocklin's fist wrapped around it came down like a hammer at the base of Gasser's skull. Gasser went down, his eyes bulging in disbelief. A few seconds later he was dead.

Rocklin put the dead man on his horse, steadied him there, and then slapped the horse sharply on the rump. Gasser's body plunged headfirst into the ground a few yards away. It wouldn't stop the questions in the minds of Fallon and his gang, but at least the town might take the death as an accident if no other cause could be found.

Buck was snorting softly and rolling his eyes when he came to Rocklin, and Rocklin had a sudden strong hunch that he was being watched. He swore softly, patted Buck soothingly, pretended to tighten his cinch, and circled to check him out, all the time scanning the terrain as far as he could see. Nothing. Well, he'd have to watch his step even more carefully now, and have a story ready in case he was confronted.

The dust was mostly around the trail where the grass was sparser; out where it was thicker there was just wind. Rocklin decided to ride out into the prairie a couple of hundred yards, circle Three Rocks, and try to pick up some sign. It wouldn't matter much if he made someone even more curious; the damage was done, and his careful check might fit into his story if he was guiltily trying to cover up an accidental death. He found nothing. Well, the day had started out in a strangely unsatisfactory way and it was running true to form. Maybe his visit with Friendly would bring results of some kind.

CHAPTER 11

Friendly's place was impressive. The ranch house was flat and spread out, not the modified eastern style with gables and narrow windows. It was more like the Spanish-style haciendas in the Southwest, unusual for the Midwest. The corrals and outhouses were some distance from the main house, and there were cottonwoods and three or four elms pleasantly spaced over the landscape.

The place suited Friendly, who turned out to be a genial host who insisted that Rocklin stay a few days. And it suited Mrs. Friendly, a serenely pleasant woman, a bit taller than her husband, strong and slender with lovely iron-gray hair. It was obvious to Rocklin that she had had a lot to do with the success and feeling of the place. He took to her at once.

"I understand that we owe you our thanks, Mr. Rocklin," she said when Friendly had introduced her, scarcely suppressing his fondness and pride.

Rocklin caught on in just a second. "Oh. Ah, it

was just . . ."

"You and Mr. . . . . Clayton, was it. . . ? must be bold and reckless men. People have died for less, now that we have the protection of Mr. Fallon's law." Her eyes, a soft brown, were direct and honest.

"It won't be long now," Friendly said, and then looked slightly flustered. Rocklin bowed to the woman and the subject was dropped. It came up again, however, when Arden Friendly strode into the room, apparently just back from a ride.

"That was short," her father remarked, and her glance flicked at Rocklin. She covered up immediately, but Rocklin thought with some relief, So that's it; the ability to dissemble doesn't come easily to a single member of the Friendly family.

"I haven't had a chance to thank you properly, Mr. Rocklin," the girl said. She was staring at him questioningly, her head slightly cocked. She might as well have told him right out that she had seen him at Three Rocks.

Rocklin smiled into her eyes. "It was nothing. Let's not speak of it again."

"All right, we won't," the girl promised.

"Let's have some lunch and then I'll show you around," Friendly said.

Rocklin and Friendly were heading north toward the Territory. The wind had finally slacked off, giving a pleasanter aspect to the day.

"You know," Friendly said, "I never connected that boy with the Texas Claytons. The word from

Fallon was that he was just a Badlands drifter looking for trouble. Nobody paid much attention to the incident. The town is used to the quick end of troublemakers. They buried the boy and that was that.

"It came as a complete surprise to me. I was up in Gridley one day and the livery-stable man asked me if I still had my visitor. Seems he was concerned because he never got his horse back. I asked him what visitor, and he told me about a young man off the train who rented a horse and asked the way to my ranch. Signed himself E. Clayton. First I had heard.

"I mentioned the incident at dinner and Arden got all upset. She said the boy had talked about coming to see her when school was out, but she hadn't really taken him seriously. I gather he was working weekends at some Central Park riding stable and that was where Arden met him. She didn't know who he was either. What was he doing working at a riding stable?

"Then I checked with Fallon. It was too much of a coincidence, a missing boy and a dead drifter. Of course, Fallon lied up one side and down the other. Claimed he didn't even know who the boy was. But he must have. A boy like that doesn't ride around in the middle of nowhere with nothing on him to tell who he is in case of trouble. A letter, initials on his gear, something. Besides, how did his brother find out about him?"

"Someone sent him an unsigned letter," Rocklin told him.

"Is that so? Huh. That could mean that someone

80

in that bunch could be on our side. Or at least against Fallon. That's interesting."

The ranch was vast, but Friendly knew where the cows were, even though they were grazing in scattered bunches. There was nothing haphazard in the way the hands kept the herds moving to different parts of the range.

"Good-looking stock," Rocklin remarked at one point. "Quite a mixture."

"Hereford, Angus, even some longhorn," Friendly said. "I have a notion the tougher strains help them get though the winters. Of course, I keep separate herds of Herefords and Angus, for breeding and for sale."

"I understand last year was a near disaster," Rocklin said.

"It was that," Friendly replied. "It was a funny thing. There must have been close to a million cows wandering the western plains from north to south, and it looked like the country was about to be hit by another panic. Beef prices dropping fast. Then winter came, the worst I've seen in these parts, and a lot of cows died. I lost a couple thousand myself. But prices steadied as a result. Some smaller outfits that couldn't afford to lose any stock at all went under, but, overall, that winter was a good thing, I think. It taught me one thing." He paused, clearly waiting to see what Rocklin would say.

"Keep some land for hay?" Rocklin asked.

Friendly shot him an appreciative glance. "You a

cowman?"

"I have a ranch in New Mexico. Not working just now. But I worked one of my own in California some years back."

Friendly was studying Rocklin. "So the act on the train was for the benefit of the man on my trail."

"I'm still looking for cattle."

"You'll get some. I've decided to thin out my herd."

"Good," Rocklin said.

"There are three things," Friendly explained. "Wild speculation in the cattle business, winter, and these damn financial panics the country seems to go through every five or ten years. I want a more manageable herd of better quality beef, feed for the winters, and enough in the bank to wait out bad times. I'll sell you ten thousand head."

"Done," Rocklin said.

"As for the mess here . . . Oh, here's my foreman. Batch!" Friendly waved to a tall, easy-riding man who had approached with four others. "Batch, I want you to meet Mr. Rocklin, who just bought ten thousand of our cows. Mr. Rocklin, Randy Batcheler, the best foreman in the business." The foreman looked both young and old, like many men who had chosen the hard and dangerous life of a cowhand. He was actually fairly young in years, but there were lines in his face that spoke of long days and nights in the saddle, pain, injury, brushes with death. When he shoved his hat back with a thumb there was a strip of fair skin between the burnt tan of his face and his hairline. But there were humor lines too, and his voice was relaxed and friendly, the kind of manner that people just naturally take to.

"I heard about your little set-to in town. Any enemy of Fallon's is a friend of mine," Batch said. "How soon are you going to need them?"

"The feeding pens will be ready in about six months," Rocklin replied.

"Where are you going?" Friendly asked his foreman.

"We're moving this bunch south a ways, toward the creek," Batch said.

"Stay clear of town," Friendly warned him.

Batch grinned and said, "For now."

"Batch," Friendly explained to Rocklin as they rode off, "is a little gone on my daughter. Well, that's all right. He's been almost like a son to me."

A little later Friendly said, "It's going to blow up, Rocklin. Sooner or later it's going sky high. More and more of my hands are going up to Gridley for their relaxation, and it's a two-day ride. So are some of the hands from the other ranches. Fallon's men go up there too. They have no say in the Territory, of course, but there have already been a couple of knock-down, drag-outs. There's bound to be a shooting sooner or later. What are you planning to do?"

"I don't know yet. Right now we have to avoid an all-out battle on Fallon's own ground, and that might not be easy. He might try to provoke one, but we can't let him. The thing is that he's making too many blunders. Things are going wrong and he's getting jumpy. That was a fool's play he made in town yesterday, and he knows it . . .

"By the way, one of the men who roughed up your daughter is the one who followed you to Chicago, Ranker by name. And you had never seen him before?"

"I don't go into town a lot anymore. Hadn't been there for six months until I went in to see about that boy who was killed. I'm not surprised Tom Clayton showed up, though. I ought to be there myself but . . . well, we had a talk, Mrs. Friendly and I . . . You see, I had told her about you. No one else, though," Friendly added quickly. "I had to lay down the law to Batch, and I guess he's wondering about things. But right now I guess I don't have much choice but to leave it in your hands, since I got you here."

The tough old-time cattleman was plainly angry and embarrassed, and Rocklin guessed there was more to that talk with his wife than he was saying. "Did your daughter actually shoot at those men?" he asked.

That was the problem, all right. Friendly hated to admit it, but he did. "Dammit, yes. Don't you think I'd have gone after those hoodlums otherwise? Regardless?"

Rocklin didn't mention that one of the hoodlums was already dead. "Well," he said, "I have a feeling Fallon's boss is going to try to make him pull in his horns, but it might be too late for that."

"His boss?"

"I'm convinced there's one man behind Fallon, an organizer with a mind that works."

"You mentioned something like that before, but I just can't imagine who it would be."

"The banker?"

"No. Willis is my own man. Hell, I brought him in and set him up."

"For various reasons, I figure the man has to be in town, or close to it. It didn't take them long at all to pick an acting marshal after Fallon blew up, for example."

"All right. Go on."

"Gerald is in the capital. I talked to him a few days ago."

"Forget Gerald. He wouldn't risk it. He wants to be governor."

"Heismann? I don't see it. Any stockman is just too busy on his ranch."

"He doesn't live too far out of town though," Friendly said. "And he lives alone. Goes into town every Friday without fail."

"He does, does he? Then he was there yesterday."

"Almost for sure."

"Is he tough enough? Smart enough?"

"I don't know," Friendly said thoughtfully. "He's tough all right, although some of that might be plain meanness. I'd say he is straight, but he just isn't the kind of man you get to know."

"Willis mentioned yesterday that he is a councilman, said the mayor was out of town. Who else is on the council?"

"It's a five-man council and the mayor's job is rotated. Right now the mayor is Con Bracken. He runs the freight office and is part owner of the line.

There's another office in Gridley and he goes up there a lot. He even drives when he's shorthanded. And he has a fine wife and seven children.

"Then there's Ollie Winslow, the blacksmith. A widower who works night and day to support a family of eleven. There's the owner of the newspaper, a sly and deceitful man . . . and there's an idea. He and his paper will always go with the power. He was with the cattlemen and the railroads until the Grange took over the state. Now he's with what he calls the little guy. He's my choice."

"That's four," Rocklin said.

"The fifth is Mildred Stocker. I gave her her start."

"I met her. A remarkable woman. How did she lose her leg?"

"A sad thing, that. A terrible thing. It was, oh I guess twelve, fifteen years ago. They were heading west with a wagon and four horses and everything else they owned. A day or so west of here they were hit by a handful of renegade Sioux. Four or five of them, they said. Probably only wanted the horses. Mildred's husband tried to outrun them and the wagon tipped over and rolled. The man was knocked cold and Midred's leg was pinned under the wagon. The Indians looted the wagon, set it afire so the people would burn alive — the kind of thing they think's funnier than hell — and made off with the horses.

"Two of my men heard the shooting, but they were a couple of miles away. When they got there, Mildred's dress was on fire and so was her husband's hair. My men could tell he had tried to pry the wagon off her leg using a rock and a singletree, but it was no use. He was cutting off her leg."

"I see," Rocklin said. "No wonder."

"My men threw a couple of ropes around the wheels sticking up in the air and tipped the wagon off her, but it would have been too late to save her leg; the leg was pretty well smashed up already. But, well . . ."

"What about her husband?"

"They're still together."

Rocklin wondered if what he was thinking was possible. "You don't mean the old man who cleans up around the place?"

"That's him."

"Interesting."

Friendly eyed him. "What's interesting about it?"

"Does she make him do it?"

"Oh no. At least I don't think so. That's a funny question. He *has* been like a whipped dog since the attack. Takes no part in the business as far as I know, just kind of hangs around and does the dirty work. Never says anything to anybody."

"You set them up?"

"Just a little store. She paid me back. She made it into the business she has today. And now the town is going to die around everyone's ears."

"Maybe not," Rocklin said. "We can stop Fallon."

"How? Anyway, it's not just Fallon. It's the railroad."

"The railroad?"

"It bypassed us. You've seen western towns bypassed by a railroad; and what happens to them?

87

They die. Sometimes overnight.

"We had a chance, but the town got greedy, figured here was a way to get rich quick. Tried to hold the railroad up for a right-of-way and the head of the company got mad and rerouted the line. Made a wide sweep clear up to Gridley. That was it. All because of a few fools and a newspaper to toot their horn every step of the way. And Andrew J. Flack . . ."

"Andrew J. Flack?"

"Flack. The owner of the newspaper. And he owned some of the land."

"So you bought some of the land the railroad abandoned?" Rocklin asked.

"No, no. That was a different road, the one that went bankrupt. This was part of that land, right here where we're riding. We're almost in the Territory now. You'll be able to spot the grade. They left some telegraph poles. See, over there about a mile. There's even track there. Receivers never did get around to pulling it up. I guess it's mine now."

"You don't say. Mind if we take a look?"

Friendly looked at Rocklin, surprised, but he obliged. "Want to buy a railroad?" he joked.

They had followed the roadbed a mile or so when they came to the end of the tracks. Everything was overgrown with grass. Rocklin dismounted and examined the rails and ties more closely.

"Not in bad shape," he remarked to Friendly. "Looks like standard gauge."

"It is," Friendly said. "It's only about four years old. What's on your mind?"

"Just a thought. Maybe a crazy one. Does this line come anywhere close to the Northern Route through Gridley?"

"You mean back down the track to the east?"

"Yes."

"Well . . . let me think a minute. Yes, it does. Twenty-five, thirty miles east it comes very close. Almost parallel for a piece. What's the idea?"

"I am thinking," Rocklin said, "of a way to meet Fallon on our own ground. Where are we right now?"

"On my land on the border between Nebraska and Dakota Territory."

"Are we in the state or the Territory?"

"Too close to tell."

"Can you have it surveyed? I mean this stretch right along here where the track ends."

"Don't see why not," Friendly said.

"Without anyone knowing?"

"I suppose so. What's on your mind?"

"A cattle town."

"A what?" Friendly was startled, and he wasn't easy to startle.

"A cattle town. *Your* cattle town. Some pens. Some loading chutes. A store and a saloon. Nothing fancy. It could be a tent town at first."

Friendly was staring at Rocklin, at first disbelieving, then thoughtful. He looked around as though seeing the area for the first time. Then he said, "And completely out of Fallon's jurisdiction."

"And completely possible," Rocklin said. "The road would connect with the Northern Route tracks where they come together, and at a very small cost, I imagine."

Friendly shook his head. "Clay Washington Major is the orneriest, most spiteful cuss who ever drew a breath. And he is president and principal stockholder of the Northern Route. He'll remember that Friendly tried to hustle him. He'll never do it."

"I've handled a couple of problems for Clay Washington Major," Rocklin said. "He'll do it. You don't ship with him now?"

"No. It's closer to Gridley, but the trail is better and there's more water driving south toward Ogallala."

"And Clay Washington Major would give his right eye to get the better of the president of that railroad. I know. I've played poker with both of them."

Friendly was trying not to show his excitement. "We can get the other ranchers together," he said. "All Gerald and Heismann have to do is make a short loop to the south and east and then head their herds straight north through my land to the railroad. It won't take them much more than a day. They'll do it. They'll go along.

"You know, Rocklin, we can take a lot of money away from that town. It'll force Fallon's hand, all right. He'll have to move against us. You've got it, Rocklin."

"The waiting game is going to be the hardest," Rocklin warned.

"I know, I know. I'll keep everybody close to home and out of trouble. We've got to keep this quiet until we're all ready. Come on, let's go home. You'll stay

90

awhile, won't you? We have to make plans."

"A little while, with pleasure. But I have to get around to other ranchers. I'm a cattle buyer, remember. Also, I have to go have a talk with Clay Washington Major."

CHAPTER 12

As soon as Tom Clayton stepped through the bat-wing doors of the saloon in Gridley he knew he had been expected. Talking stopped; faces turned his way.

He looked around and thought, Word travels fast. I wonder which of them are Fallon's men. By the time he reached the bar he had decided they were the four at the last table in the far corner of the room. Why? He wasn't sure. Maybe, he thought, it's simply that they don't look like regular townspeople or working cowhands.

He picked a spot at the bar opposite the four men at the table, nodded when the barman asked him if he wanted a whiskey, accepted a bottle and a glass, poured a drink and tossed it down.

"My name's Tom Clayton," he said to the barman in a conversational way. "Maybe you can help me. I'm looking for a man named Bill Dosser. He was one of Jack Fallon's so-called lawmen in the town of Friendly."

Without even knowing he did it, the barman

glanced at the men in the corner. "Why?" he asked.

"He and two other of these so-called lawmen killed my brother. One of the three, name of Yates, was killed south of Friendly. I was told a man named Dusty Kitt was knifed to death here in Gridley. That leaves Dosser."

"I haven't seen him for three, four weeks," the barman said. "Last I heard he lit out for the Black Hills." It was very quiet in the place; every man present could hear what was being said. Clayton poured himself another shot, turned to the room and asked, "Anyone here know where the man might be?"

A pockmarked hardcase at the corner table pushed his chair back, and the scraping sound was loud in the room. "Why don't you ask his brother," he grated. His eyes glittered and his right hand was beneath the tabletop. "He's sitting right here."

Clayton regarded him. "You?" he asked.

"Me."

"Hold it!" Another man at the table stood up and Clayton could see he was wearing a badge under his coat. He headed for the bar, but he was going to Clayton's right. With the slightest of motions, Clayton waved him to his left, away from his gun hand, and the lawman obliged. "I'm sheriff of this county, and if you have any business with me we'll talk in my office."

"Are you on Fallon's payroll?" Clayton asked. The man went white around the lips and his hand rested on the six-shooter on his hip. Clayton cocked his head slightly at the sheriff, let his gaze switch down to the gun and then back up, with a question in it. It said as plain as words, "If you're going to do it, do it." It was a trick Clayton had of avoiding the promiscuous use of firearms, and he himself didn't know exactly how it worked. All he knew for sure was that part of it was not challenging a man out loud where everyone could hear.

The sheriff was mad clear through. "I'm on the payroll of this county, and if Lonny Dosser draws that gun he'll answer to me. And if you want . . ." Lonny Dosser drew the gun. First, though, he pushed his chair back a little farther from the table, and again the scrape echoed loudly in the room.

Tom Clayton was all muscle and nerve. And despite a lifetime of brutally hard work, his reactions were as quick as a honkytonk banjo player's. As he reacted now, it was as though his mind, but only his mind, went into slow and deliberate motion. He saw Dosser's clear intent to kill him. But he also saw the man to Dosser's right at the table, a man with a long bony face who seemed to be gazing with sleepy eyes at the top of the table but whose hands were out of sight beneath it. Clayton drew his .44 and shot the sleepy man full in the chest and the man's shot from under the table blasted a hole in the floor. The man on Sleepy's right was trying to make up his mind whether he wanted part of this or not. Dosser's gun was coming up, and for an instant he was half standing there dead when the lead from Clayton's gun burst into fragments going through his breastbone and tore up his heart and his lungs. Then he sat down in the chair again and fell sideways to the floor. The third man had made up his mind and then changed it, too late; he hesitated. Clayton saw the hesitation and held his fire, but the sheriff, who didn't perceive things in slow motion, shot the man between the eyes.

As the smoke was settling, the sheriff turned to Clayton, speaking rapidly. "All right, we were on the same side and you're in the clear. But I'll have to watch my back every second from now on. Try the old water stop to the east. It's not in my county. Get going." Clayton didn't hesitate. Before the barman had crawled up off the floor behind his bar, he was on the other side of the flapping doors.

He was hardly out of town, following wagon-wheel ruts alongside the railroad tracks, when he caught the sound of hooves behind him, then a low whistle. He swiveled his mount and waited, his hand on his gun. It was Rocklin.

"Heading my way?" Clayton asked.

"Nope. Heading east as soon as my train comes." Clayton nodded, but asked no questions. "I have an idea how to bring this mess to a head," Rocklin volunteered. "I'll be back." Clayton was in a hurry, but he knew Rocklin wouldn't have stopped him unless he had some reason.

"I heard some shooting back in town. You?"

Clayton nodded. "The brother of the man who shot Ellis. Now I'm going after the third and last."

"Did someone point you in this direction?" Rocklin asked.

"The sheriff. Why?"

"Ranker was in town earlier. He got there about an hour before you did. I saw him talking to the sheriff. Then he headed down this same trail. His arm is bandaged and in a sling, but he can still shoot a rifle. Did you happen to get the idea that somebody in Gridley knew you were coming?"

Clayton nodded thoughtfully. "I did. I saw a rider a few miles out and he seemed to be in a hurry. He came from nowhere out of the southwest. I wondered if he was making a wide sweep to get into town ahead of me. But why? Nobody knew where I was going."

"They knew you'd go looking for Bill Dosser. Somebody did, anyhow. And there's that lookout on the water tower."

"Yeah. I didn't even think of that. Thanks, Rocklin." He started to turn and stopped. "On the other hand, the sheriff backed me in the gunplay."

"Well," Rocklin said, "nothing's simple around here. See you in a few days."

"I'll be around."

CHAPTER 13

Mary Tillman
17 Washington Square Place
New York City, New York

My dearest wife,

I am writing this on a train bound for Chicago. I will mail it when I get there and I only wish I could bring it to you myself. To tell the truth I was seriously tempted to do just that — the job would keep for a few days — but the real problem would be leaving again once I got home. To tell the truth again, I am enjoying being out of the city, and I was wondering if we might take the children and spend next winter in New Mexico. Well, think about it.

This is probably the most interesting, and touchiest, situation I have ever had to deal with. I won't tell you too much about it now, but one unusual thing is that I think I have the solution before I have fully defined the problem. I can tell you that as part of the solution, I am going to Chicago to talk a man into opening a railroad! Also, the man I am dealing directly with in Nebraska is going to start a town! He is a seasoned old rancher (perhaps he looks older than he is) and he is just plain excited. He is already having the site surveyed and a well dug, and as soon as the railroad opens up (tracks are in place) material will start coming in for pens and chutes and a few buildings. He says he wants to call it Alice Junction after his wife.

The key part of the problem that I have not defined is: Who is behind the trouble in Friendly? I have met and talked to just about everybody who might be, but I don't have an inkling. All I have at this point is a couple of hunches that are too wild to waste much time on.

Do you remember old Quigley? He was a neighbor out in California. I met a man named Heismann yesterday who is so much like him they could be twins. Pious and penurious, we called Quigley, and this man is just the same; only Quigley was a good man at heart despite his pinch-penny ways, and I'm not so sure about Heismann. He is a lifelong bachelor and, to put it kindly, has few of the social graces. His spread is impeccably neat, however, and the bunkhouse is spacious and comfortable. On the other hand, any man caught smoking, drinking, gambling, fighting, or taking the Lord's name in vain is fired on the spot. I am told that almost no one ever quits. Nothing is more interesting than people, don't you agree?

I think I can promise that I won't be away longer than a month, but I won't promise any less. You will be pleased to know that you distract my thoughts oftener than I should let you. Give my love to the children.

I remain
Your loving husband,
William R. Tillman

CHAPTER 14

Tom Clayton stopped to take in the country and decide what to do. The railroad tracks were veering southeast toward the flatter grassland. But Ranker's trail turned slightly north through a stretch of low sand hills, where there were better spots for an ambush.

On the other hand, Ranker knew Clayton wasn't blind and he had made no effort to cover his tracks. What was he thinking? Clayton reached for his saddlebags and took out a pair of glasses. He studied the prairie as far along the tracks as he could see. The binoculars helped, but it was next to impossible to spot all the dips and rises under the blowing grass. Tricky territory. Trickier in a way than the sand hills because in the rougher country a careful man would instinctively ride clear of possible ambushes.

Clayton decided that Ranker wanted him to follow the railroad tracks, so instead he followed the trail into the sand hills. He was still following it when it dipped slightly into a rocky defile where tough clumps of bunch grass gave him some cover. He dismounted and crawled up the side of the defile to again scan the area to the south. To his surprise, the land just below him had turned flat again and the railroad had apparently curved toward north of east; it was there, hardly a half-mile away. Which meant . . .

Clayton settled down flat on his vantage point for a long hard look at what was around him. If Ranker was laying for him, and he almost certainly was, this had to be pretty close to the place. To the east, the rough country was smoothing out. Farther along, the railroad tracks were curving more sharply southeast and the grass was higher. He was trying to follow the direction of the tracks when he spotted the old water tower and, just to the north of it, a weatherbeaten shack.

So where was Ranker? He had to be around here someplace because he knew the lay of the land and this was obviously the best place to be. He had set it up so he could pick Clayton off whichever way he came.

As he searched every foot of ground he could see with his glasses, Clayton thought about Bill Dosser, the man in the shack, and how he could approach him without being seen. The simple answer was that he would have to go in after dark. The sun would be gone in a couple of hours. And what if he found Ranker? If there was shooting, the wind would carry the sound straight to the shack. Would Dosser be curious enough to lie low and wait? Or would he immediately take off for tall timber? If he did it

101

might take another year to track him down. And, Clayton wondered, where is the man's horse? He searched the area around the shack again. The horse wasn't in the shade of the water tower. It wasn't on the other side of the shack; the place was too small to hide a horse. So Dosser was already gone, or there was a low spot out there in all that grass. Which meant there *might* be a way to approach the shack without being seen.

But where was Ranker? What if Ranker had caught a glimpse of him on the higher trail and doubled back to meet him. Clayton had a sudden urge to move. He dropped the glasses, rolled over swiftly, and pulled out his .44. He saw a movement just below him, not fifty yards away, and fired . . .

Ranker had gotten impatient. He had raised up between two dunes that looked like only one to see what was keeping Clayton. He had spotted Clayton about an hour earlier on the higher trail and hadn't been all that surprised. He would have had an easier, clearer shot at Clayton if he had come down the tracks, but it didn't matter all that much. All he had to do was wait. Then he had started wondering if Clayton had circled farther to the north and then back. The conviction grew on Ranker that he was in the wrong place. It had been too long. He had better move.

As he stood up, Clayton's slug creased his scalp and tore his hat off. At least he had the advantage of a rifle over a six-shooter. He whirled and fired at the top of the small rise just as Clayton ducked behind it, but before he could cock his Winchester again

Clayton shot the top of his head off.

Clayton was going over to make sure when he heard three shots, evenly spaced. He thought it over and decided it was a helluva coincidence but he would take a chance on it anyway. The shots had sounded just like a signal and, if so, someone had taken the three shots he and Ranker had fired as a signal. It was too lucky not to be true. He decided to ride right up the tracks to the hideout while there was still daylight.

Bill Dosser watched through the peephole in the door as Clayton approached and then stepped out with his rifle, cocked and ready, cradled in his arm. "Stop right there," he told Clayton. "I don't know you. Who told you the signal?"

"I'm new around here," Clayton said. "I came to give you a message. Your brother's dead."

"Dead? How?"

"He was shot by Tom Clayton. Do you know who Tom Clayton is?"

"I know about him. I'll ask you just once more. Who are you?"

"I'm Tom Clayton."

It took a second for it to register and a split second for Dosser's rifle to come up, but that was much too late.

Clayton pulled up at the Friendly roadblock and waited for the two sentries to say something. It took them awhile to think of anything, but then one of them drew a gun and said, "Stay right where you are.

103

Don't move." He went cautiously around to the two horses Clayton was leading and examined the bodies hanging across the saddles. "It's Ranker and Bill Dosser," he said to his partner. His partner drew a gun and ordered Clayton to unbuckle his gunbelt and drop it.

Clayton favored the man with a thin smile and said, "Why? I'm just delivering a couple of your boss's men. They ran into trouble up in the Territory. It has nothing to do with you." From the corner of his eye Clayton saw the rider who had been dogging him for the last couple of miles draw closer. It was Arden Friendly.

The man who had examined the bodies rejoined his partner in the middle of the road. "You killed them?" he asked.

"I did."

"We'll take care of them. This isn't Texas. We're the law here."

Clayton's smile grew thinner and he looked the two men insolently up and down. "The law here killed my brother."

"*We* didn't kill your brother," said the man who was doing the talking. "And Friendly has a law: Nobody wears a gun into town."

Arden Friendly was coming closer and listening. The second man said, "You move along, Miss Friendly. This isn't your affair."

"I believe I'm outside the township on my father's ranch," she said.

"I have to take your gun. It's the law," the first man insisted.

Clayton leaned forward in his saddle and spoke patiently as though to children. "When I first rode into town, Ranker started a ruckus about that very thing."

There was silence as the two men made the connection. It was true. And now Ranker was hanging dead over his saddle.

The second man said, "Why don't we ride in with him and let Fallon handle it."

"Because we're in charge here and now," the spokesman said. But he moved aside to let Clayton pass and his partner followed suit. Clayton started between the men, then hesitated and nudged his horse to a stop. He took off his gunbelt, handed it to the surprised spokesman, and rode on through.

Everybody in town turned out to watch the procession approach the marshal's office. Willis emerged from his bank and stood there as though frozen in shock. Old man Stocker was sweeping the walk in front of the hotel and store and was presently joined by Mildred. They watched, expressionless. Flack, the publisher, ran up the street from his office, stopped dead-still and looked as though he was trying to work up enough nerve to ask a question. Fallon looked out over the swinging doors of the saloon, scowled, then stepped through the doors and walked slowly up the walk to the marshal's office. He was there, standing beside Jackson, as Clayton and the two deputies pulled up. Arden Friendly was sitting on her horse across the street.

The first person to speak was Jackson. "Well?" he demanded of his deputies.

"It's Ranker and Bill Dosser," the spokesman said.

"I can see who they are."

"He said he killed them up in the Territory."

Jackson looked at Clayton. "Where in the Territory?"

"At the old water stop east of Gridley."

"That's in Bolling County. Why bring them here?"

"The county seat was too far." He looked directly at Fallon. "Besides, they were Fallon's men. I figured he'd know what to do with them."

Fallon was pale with anger. "I know what to do with you." He was wearing a gun and a deputy's badge, and he was within a fraction of a second of being out of control.

Clayton, unarmed, decided to push him. He laughed without humor and said, "You'll get your chance. The men who did the actual killing are dead. But you were the man responsible." He looked around at the crowd and then back at Fallon. "You'll be seeing me at the right time and place."

Fallon was so unhinged with frustration and rage that some of the onlookers backed away from him, and Jackson, alarmed, started to urge him to take it easy. Then Flack spoke up, his high-pitched voice full of nerves.

"What about Lonny Dosser, Clayton? He had nothing to do with it?"

Clayton ignored the newsman. "I'm leaving now. I'll thank you for my gun," he said to the two deputies.

"We'll ride out with you," the spokesman said.

"Wait a minute," Jackson barked. "What about

these bodies? They don't belong to us."

"They belong to Fallon," Clayton said, then he rode out of town.

The next morning Andrew J. Flack's *Clarion* carried a front-page editorial that said in part:

Tom Clayton is the prototype of the ruthless and arrogant cattle baron who for years has trampled the rights of the common people under the hooves of his ubiquitous herds.

In his unslaked thirst for vengeance, Clayton has killed three, and possibly four, law officers of this community, and has had the temerity literally to dump them on our doorstep and ride away.

Well, we have news for Tom Clayton and all of his ilk: This community rose up once before and established laws — a code of civilized behavior, if you will — that have brought a long period of peace and security. AND WE CAN DO IT AGAIN.

CHAPTER 15

Clayton watched Arden Friendly as she settled her horse, a beautiful dappled gray, into an easy gallop and put distance between herself and him. He lost sight of her a time or two and realized again that the terrain was not as even as it looked. For someone who knew the lay of the land there were plenty of hiding places. His mind drifted to other things and after a while he became aware that he had lost sight of her altogether. When he sighted Three Rocks he thought about circling around it but decided not to. He knew he was making enemies he didn't even know about, but instinct told him it was too soon to start watching every move he made. Besides, he was a direct man who had always smoked out trouble as soon as he smelled it, and more than once had caught it by surprise. It was his way, and if he had ever thought about it he had seen no reason to change.

So he was more exasperated than anything when

his horse signaled that there was something more at Three Rocks than just the rocks. He maintained his steady approach but pulled his rifle from the saddle holster and cradled it in his right arm. He heard a horse whinny but kept going. Anyone could have stopped on the shady side of the rocks to give his horse a rest.

He rode in, circled the first rock, and found Arden Friendly standing by her gray looking up at him. He was surprised but didn't show it. He stopped and gazed down at her, waiting for her to speak, studying her face.

It was a small face, well shaped and alive with color. Stubbornness around her mouth and a slightly too pointed nose. It made her look snooty. Intelligent eyes of golden brown and lots of hair of exactly the same color. An attractive face, if its owner could relax it just a little.

"Why did you give them your gun?" the girl demanded. "If you had kept it, Fallon would have tried to kill you and you could have killed him."

Clayton eyed her for another moment, wondering what this thing was about Fallon. Then he very deliberately dismounted and placed himself close in front of her, looking down at her high color. She returned his gaze defiantly, refusing to move. "You were all that much in love, then?" he asked.

Her color deepened but she stood her ground. "What does that have to do with it? He was fun. And I liked him a lot. He was your *brother.*"

"Did he ask you to marry him?" Clayton insisted. "Yes."

"And how did you feel?"

Her blush, which had subsided, rose again in her cheeks. "I don't know," she replied with forthright honesty. Then, realizing the answer sounded weak, even to her, she snapped, "You are on my father's ranch. Why?"

"He invited me. At my convenience, he said."

"Oh. Well then, of course you are welcome. Excuse me." She started to turn away, but Clayton decided to give in to an urge he had had ever since he climbed down from his horse. He wrapped his arms around her and kissed her very emphatically on her lips. She didn't resist, nor did she cooperate, exactly. To Clayton's astonishment she seemed to be . . . well, *analyzing* the experience.

When he released her, the golden brown eyes searched his disconcertingly and she said, "Why did you do that?"

He drew back, half amused, looked at her more carefully, and said, "You don't mean that."

"Don't you know?"

"Of course I know. But you are the most surprising . . ."

"Then why?" Clayton stalled. "So you won't answer." She had an odd expression, as if he had disappointed her. If it was a game it was a new one on Clayton, and in fact he didn't really think it was.

"All right," he said. "The wind was blowing your hair. Your face was flushed. You looked tense and beautiful and very alive. And you were in reaching distance. Is that enough?"

"And there was no other reason?"

"I don't understand. What other reason could there be? You were there. Now you answer my question. Isn't that enough?"

"And that I am the daughter of the rich and powerful Hanson Friendly has nothing to do with it?"

"Ah. Yes, of course. I see. Has it been that bad for you? I'm sorry." There was a glint of anger in her eyes and they turned darker, but he pretended not to notice. "Don't try to tell me that was my brother's reaction, because I know better."

"He didn't know that much about me. I can make friends with people who don't know much about me. And I . . ." She bit it off.

"And you don't have any friends." It was a flat statement and she resented it. Again she started to turn away, but he caught her arm. "No you don't. You started this, and it's nowhere near finished."

"Let me go."

He released her arm and said, "So you can only take your honesty in small doses." She didn't move but only stared at him. "So you would rather be some girl from the town whose father is a poor dirt farmer. Do you think that would make a difference? Do you think *you* would be different? Well?"

"Of course I would," she retorted. Then she paused and looked thoughtful. "In some ways."

"And in other ways?" he pressed.

"Well . . . naturally, of course I wouldn't."

"That's right. *Naturally.* Because of your nature."

"It isn't that simple," Arden Friendly said.

"No. Of course it isn't. When you're made to feel

different . . ."

Tom Clayton felt a small ache in his heart. He recognized it for what it was; he had felt it before, even as a child, and he remembered his surprise to find that a heart could actually ache, just like songs and poems said it could. It had to do with . . . it had to do with something about other people . . . strangers.

"So as long as you are naturally yourself, would you rather be poor than rich?" he insisted.

She thought about it at some length and then said, "Yes and no."

Clayton laughed, without derision. "That," he said, "could be the true answer to all the questions people have ever asked themselves. But I think I know what you mean."

Without any further communication they turned and started walking slowly down the trail, leading their horses. They had walked in silence as much as a mile when Arden said, "All right, Tom Clayton, how did *you* handle it?"

He chuckled. "You know, I was just thinking about that. It took awhile, of course, but finally I just decided not to handle it at all. I'm not sure anyone is ever accepted for just what he is, but when you are . . . well, when your father is . . . *the* power in his part of the country, people know it. Even kids know it. And everyone lets you know that they know, in one way or another.

"And do you know what I did? I watched my dad. He was a man who had tried an impossible thing, and had done it. Your father is the same way. It

112

shows. They don't live in the same world that everyone else lives in. They have made their own world, and they . . . uh, well, they sort of carry it around with them.

"Maybe it's harder for you because you're a woman. But you see, a man has his work, and when that work is everything, nothing makes any difference. His family, of course, is part of his work, but . . . well, I suppose it's the same with women, but they aren't out in the middle of things where they are forced by others to deal with . . . things."

There was another long silence. They seemed to decide at the same moment that it was time to ride again.

"I think my dad is out at the railroad," Arden said. "There's already a lot going on out there. I'll ride along and show you the trail, if you'd like."

"I would be much obliged," Clayton said.

CHAPTER 16

Rocklin suspected he had run into another obstacle as soon as he saw the young man at the desk, and he was in no mood for it. It had taken him long enough to get the railroad telegrapher in Gridley to find out just where Clay Washington Major was. He had been sorely tried then and had wanted to shove his gun down the telegrapher's throat, but had finally convinced the man that Clay Washington Major would be very upset if he found out Rocklin wanted to see him and the telegrapher had not cooperated. After much signaling back and forth, it was discovered that Clay Washington Major was not at the railhead, or out on the line somewhere in his private car, or in the head office in Omaha. He was in his Chicago office. Now Rocklin was in the Chicago office, and there in front of him was the obstacle.

"Your name?" the young man asked. He had a tight, efficient mouth, wore a high, stiff collar, an embroidered vest made of slipper satin, and sleeve garters.

"Rocklin."

"You don't have an appointment," the young man accused.

"Would you mind telling him I am here."

"He is in a meeting. You will have to make an appointment for some time tomorrow."

"Maybe if you just whispered to him that I am here," Rocklin suggested.

"I can't do that. I told you he is in a meeting."

Rocklin leaned forward slightly. "And I am telling you that your boss is going to tear a strip of hide off of you six inches wide from top to bottom. Then it will be my turn. The name is Rocklin."

The young man was all right. He turned slightly pink but rose with dignity and said, "Just a minute, sir." Rocklin thought with amusement that he would probably go far.

Clay Washington Major burst out of his office followed by half a dozen railroad men. He was wearing an old suit of dark blue wool and his tie was askew, but his weathered old face with its droopy mustache was as tough-looking as ever and his eyes were as acquisitive.

"All right," he was saying, "get on with it, and I'll be out at the railhead in a couple of weeks." Without taking a breath he said, "Rocklin. Why didn't you let me know you were here? Come in,

115

come on in. I hear you had a little trouble locating me."

"How did you hear that?" Rocklin asked. "I made no complaints."

"I know everything that goes on on my railroads. Sit down. The last time we got together you took me for five thousand dollars. Are you going to give me a chance to get some of it back?"

"Not this time. I hear you're at the Snake."

"We'll be across in about a month. What were you doing in Dakota?"

"Well now, there I have a little problem."

"You always do. Still troubleshooting for the Cattlemen's Association, huh?"

"You don't know that, dammit."

"Know what? I forgot what I said." He laughed heartily at the joke. "All right, if I can help I will. I owe you for what you did. I always will, confound you." He laughed again. "What is it?"

"I want to offer you a few miles of railroad." Clay Washington Major was not easy to astonish, but he drew back slightly and his eyes narrowed. He knew, and Rocklin knew, that Rocklin would get what he came for, but that didn't mean there would be no tough poker.

"Right now? You're crazy. Don't you know I have to reach the West Coast before winter. Not a chance."

"Not more than thirty miles of track and it's already in place. All it will take is some switching and a side track and of course a thorough check of the roadbed. It hasn't had a train on it since it was

116

built. The whole thing is just sitting there, a ready-made branch. Does it ring a bell?"

"It does. The Nebraska and Western bankruptcy. It was a bad idea in the first place. Do you mean the receivers haven't gotten around to pulling up the track?"

"Yes. They haven't. You could get it for practically nothing."

"What do I want with it?"

"Do you know Hanson Friendly?"

"I've met him. That damn town of his tried to hold me up."

"And you got even," Rocklin pointed out.

"I always do. I'm not going to ask you what this is all about."

"I appreciate it. You probably know that Hanson and a rancher named Sykes Heismann and Senator Ed Gerald drive south to Ogallala instead of north to Gridley because it's an easier trail and because there's more water . . ."

"So John J. Hargreaves gets the business," said Clay Washington Major with a deep scowl.

"Right," Rocklin said with a grin. "And a good bit of business it is. But suppose you had a branch right there on Friendly's property? I suppose you know about Shafter's new plant in Minnesota." Clay Washington Major nodded. "I'm buying most of the beef from those three ranches."

"I know of Heismann. Never met him. But I've met Senator Kenworth, called Ed, Gerald. He wouldn't give me a glass of warm spit in hell."

"He may not have much choice. It's getting

pretty crowded with farms around the Platte and the North Platte. One of these days they might not be able to get a herd through to Ogallala."

"So they'll have to go to Gridley whether they want to or not. Why should I make it any easier for them? And you said the branch would be on Friendly's property. Do you mean he owns the land?"

"I'm surprised you missed that. Yes. He bought it from the receivers."

"And you expect me to operate a railroad, even a branch of a railroad, on land I don't own? You're crazier than I thought, Rocklin."

"You can have a ninety-nine year lease. Renewable."

"I'll take every other section on both sides of the right-of-way clear to the end of the line."

"A lease," Rocklin insisted.

"I won't do it. You're asking too much. All right, I know I owe you, but this is *business*. The answer is no."

Rocklin showed his hole card. "Well, all right. I thought I'd give you first shot at it. It's a natural for you, right there within a mile of your tracks. Very little outlay and a good steady return." He got up to go.

"Sit down!" Clay Washington Major yelled. "What do you mean, first shot at it?"

"Well," Rocklin drawled, "I thought as long as I'm in Chicago I might drop in for a talk with John J."

Red-necked fury at first, then an idea and a sly

118

look of victory. Clay Washington Major had his own hole card. "Oh you did, did you? And just where will Hargreaves connect this branch out in the middle of nowhere? Not to *my* line."

"You forget his Kansas City and Western."

"Ridiculous. He'd have to lay a hundred miles of track. The damn skinflint would never do it. You're talking through your hat, Rocklin."

"Not even to drive a line into your territory? I think he'd go a lot further than that to stick a thorn in your side."

"You're a damn scoundrel, Rocklin." Now Clay Washington Major was really yelling. "You might as well have let them hang me ten years ago."

The young man at the desk looked ridiculously startled when the boss and his visitor came through the door.

"And don't come back. We're quits," a red-faced Clay Washington Major was saying. "I'll have a crew out there within a week."

CHAPTER 17

Rocklin didn't like the feeling of the town of Friendly. Neither did Buck, whose head bounced up a couple of times as his ears and nostrils tested the atmosphere. Rocklin, in a gesture he was not aware of, leaned forward and patted his horse on the side of his neck in acknowledgment. The man and the horse communicated with each other in uncanny ways that had settled more or less into habit, and they relied on each other implicitly. It was one of the main reasons that Rocklin always approached a job with a few days' trip across country, to give himself and Buck a chance to shed their city senses and sharpen their reactions to wilder territory, where the difference between the slower pace of life and the swifter disasters could demand constant attention.

Rocklin drew up in front of the hotel, where he had kept his room, and threw Buck's reins over the hitching rail. Newton Stocker, who was at his seemingly ceaseless sweeping, came over to take the horse to the livery stable.

Rocklin had been thinking about the Stockers, and the more he thought the weirder the situation seemed. He decided to test the man. He looked directly at him and said, "Thank you, Mr. Stocker. Fine day. Not so windy." The man's eyes darted up to Rocklin's face and down again, and the glance was anything but dull. He shook his head slightly and led Buck quickly away.

As he entered the hotel, Rocklin saw Mildred Stocker leaning on a crutch and watching him from the doorway of the general store. He gave a little wave and wished her good morning and she smiled her twisted smile and waved back.

The desk man at the hotel left his paperwork just long enough to hand Rocklin his key. He didn't reply when Rocklin said good morning. Rocklin thought he could guess what had happened. The work on the branch and the new town was known, of course, and talk had gotten around that he had had something to do with it. It was inevitable and he had expected it, but it made things more difficult. When he had treated himself to a bath and a change of clothes he went down to eat, and the first person he ran into was the banker, Brandon Willis.

Willis was uncharacteristically direct when he saw Rocklin. He came across the hotel lobby and invited himself to lunch, and when they were seated he came right out with it.

"I hear you had something to do with Friendly's branch railroad," he said in an accusing voice.

"Something, yes," Rocklin said, "although it isn't

exactly Friendly's. It's Clay Washington Major's. And believe me it took some talking."

The answer took Willis by surprise. He didn't speak for a moment, then he said, "So you've weighed in on Friendly's side."

"On Friendly's side?" The small dining room had gone suddenly quiet. "I don't get you. Has something been going on while I was out of town?"

"*Talk* has been going on," Willis said, "that Friendly plans to go into competition with his own town, that he has threatened to close it down."

"Oh, talk. Is that all? You should know about talk, Mr. Willis. There are times in an isolated corner of the world like this one that there is nothing else to do.

"Anyhow, the branch was *my* idea. Shafter is going to need a heavy and steady flow of beef, and pigs and sheep for that matter. It'll be cheaper for the ranchers to get their stock to the railroad, so they'll make more money. It will probably lower the price at the packing plant eventually, so Shafter will make more money. And Major will make more money. When he sees how much more, he will probably extend the branch into Friendly. It's good for everyone."

"Major will never do it," Willis argued. "He swore he wouldn't. He says we tried to cheat him."

"Don't kid yourself," Rocklin said. "If there's enough money in it he will do it." He decided to press a little. "Speaking of talk, I've heard that the politicians in town did try to hold him up."

"That's not true. It's just that . . ." The banker, aware of ears all around, decided to choose his

122

words. "Well, some people didn't really want the railroad. They thought it would spoil the town." He paused to think and added, "And I can understand how they felt."

"And also," Rocklin prodded, "the men who run the town didn't want any outsiders interfering with their sweet little deal. Or so I've heard. Talk, again." From two or three corners of the room Rocklin heard some stifled laughter.

Willis looked a bit hot under the collar. "The council runs the town, and I'll tell you it's an honest council. And you happen to be talking to the mayor."

"Oh. The job has rotated to you?"

"Last Tuesday."

"Congratulations. But I wasn't talking about the council. I was talking about Fallon's so-called protective league . . . Now wait a minute, don't jump through the ceiling. I know it's just talk. You know, like the talk that Friendly is going to shut down his own town. But I've heard whispers that Fallon doesn't actually run things, that there's a mastermind behind everything. You see? When folks have nothing better to do they make things up."

The look on the banker's face was a study. Indignation, yes; denial, yes, but also a funny look, as if a new and startling thought had crossed his mind. He wasn't acting. He couldn't have been. He wasn't that clever. While he and Rocklin were finishing their meal in silence two men who were strangers to Rocklin paid their bill and left. They were wearing shiny new deputy badges. The fat was in the fire.

A little while later Rocklin decided to drop in and compliment Flack on his hard-hitting editorial, a copy of which he had found in the restaurant.

Arden Friendly, her body stiff with anger, was standing at the counter of the combination office and print shop glaring at the publisher.

"You can't possibly expect me to run this," Flack was saying to her. He looked beside himself.

"Why not," she demanded. "It's a paid advertisement. You're in the business of selling advertising, aren't you?"

"But you call me a liar and a toady, among other things," the publisher yelled. "You're . . ."

"It's truer than that slander you printed."

"You're crazy, Miss Friendly. Do you know that. The death of your friend has unhinged you. Now get out of my newspaper."

"Good afternoon," Rocklin said. Both of them turned to him as though they hadn't seen him standing there.

"You certainly cooked yourself in this town," Flack railed at him.

"What do you mean?" Rocklin asked.

"Saying what you did about the police force." He was not yelling now, but his voice was high-pitched and grating.

"What? That? Why I was just repeating what I thought was common gossip. We were talking about gossip."

"I don't believe it," Flack said between his teeth. "Nobody talks like that in this town. I mean . . . I mean . . ."

124

Rocklin smiled. "I think I know what you mean."

"No. I didn't mean . . ."

Arden Friendly put all the contempt she could muster into her voice, and it was plenty. "Then I'll take it to Gridley and get it printed. And I'll post it on every building in this town. And in Gridley too."

Rocklin followed her out of the newspaper office and had to step quickly aside when she slammed the door.

"What are you smiling at?" She almost spit it at him. "There's nothing to smile about. Especially for you. Your life's not worth a nickel now."

"Tell me, Miss Friendly, who would you pick as the kingpin in this town?"

"Are you a fool? Asking me something like that right out here in the middle of the street? Are you trying to commit suicide?"

"We're just passing the time of day. I have dealings with your father, remember? If we sought privacy, that would be noticed. Try to collect your wits and just stroll along with me for a piece. It was a serious question."

She lowered her voice, but there was just as much venom in it. "Andrew J. Flack."

"No. Didn't you see his reaction? Impossible. He's a nitwit. Now think."

She was silent for a while as they walked toward the hotel. Then she said, "You're working for my father, aren't you?"

Rocklin would gladly have throttled her. "Your father is a cattleman," he said. "I'm a cattle buyer.

What I accomplish here is important to many people, including Hanson Friendly. Turmoil here could mean turmoil for me and the company I buy for. We're talking about the future. You are not helping your father by throwing childish fits."

He thought for a second that she was going to turn on him with her claws, but he had underestimated her. She brought her anger under control, stared at him intently, and then started laughing.

"What are you, Rocklin, really?" she teased. "And how did you manage to kill Gasser Mann?"

Rocklin ignored the questions. "Who would it be? Someone who is smart enough and ruthless enough?"

"People are saying it was an accident, you know. Gasser wasn't exactly famous for his horsemanship."

"I asked you a serious question."

"I don't know. I hadn't thought along those lines until I heard what you said in the restaurant. I'm not sure anyone had. But they surely are now; you can depend on that."

"What do you think of Mildred Stocker?" Rocklin asked.

"I think she is the awfulest person I know. The way she treats her husband . . . do you know he sleeps in the shed out back? She could be the one all right. How did you ever think of that? Don't you know that all women west of the Missouri are as pure as they are courageous and beautiful?"

It was Rocklin's turn to laugh. "You're too young for that kind of talk. What did they teach you at that eastern school, anyway."

126

"What do you know about that?"

"I hear a lot in my business. Besides, it came up when I was visiting, remember?"

"But you don't say a lot, except on purpose. Tell me, Mr. Rocklin, whoever you are," she took his arm and slanted her remarkable eyes up at him, "are you married?"

"None of your business. And you don't need another father."

She laughed at him and actually snuggled against his side, and he was thinking that this was a most complex girl. She surprised him again by saying, "But how could she control Fallon?"

"I don't know. She would probably have to have a hold over him in some way."

They saw Marshal Jackson bearing down on them from the hotel entrance.

The girl disengaged herself and said, "Well, Mr. No Name Rocklin, I hope you stay alive for a while because I'm beginning to like you. But I doubt it."

"And I hope you stay out of mischief," Rocklin said.

Jackson's manner was very official as he approached. His voice was loud with the confidence that he was in charge. He was acting like Fallon. "I've been looking for you, Rocklin. We're going to have a little talk."

"Good day, Mr. Rocklin," Arden Friendly said.

"At your service, Marshal," Rocklin said cheerfully.

"In here." Jackson steered him toward the table in the back corner of the saloon, and when he had waved the bartender away he didn't mince words. "You're a troublemaker, Rocklin. I want you out of town."

"My business is almost finished," Rocklin assured him. "I'll be leaving in a few days."

"You have too much business. You're leaving today."

Rocklin was tipped back, balancing his chair on two legs and looking casually around the saloon. Something was nagging at him. They were alone. The bartender, a defeated man who was slowly drinking himself to death, had shuffled away. The back corner was private, all right, but . . . Rocklin remembered Jackson's voice growling, "I do business in my office."

"I thought Friendly was a law-abiding town." Rocklin was looking at a stovepipe hole high up in the wall opposite. There was no brass lid; the hole was just there. Apparently a pot-bellied stove replaced the poker table in the winter.

"It is a law-abiding town," Jackson rasped. "And it's going to stay that way."

"What kind of law?" Rocklin was just asking, not arguing. "Has Friendly seceded? Usually in the United States people aren't ordered around by public servants unless they've done something."

"You've disturbed the peace in this town."

"Oh? How?"

"You know how. This town is split wide open, and you did it on purpose. Why? What's your game?"

"You know I came here to buy cattle. Didn't your boss have someone check on me?"

"Fallon has nothing to do with this. Forget him. I'm the marshal now. And by the way, everybody knows that Gasser Mann was laying for you, and the next thing anyone knows, he's dead. What about it?"

"Don't ask me. And I didn't mean Fallon."

"That's it. I heard you said something like that. You're loco. What are you trying to do?"

"Come on, Jackson. You've shown a little sense a time or two. Don't tell me you haven't wondered about things around here." Jackson was silent, glaring. "Let me ask you something. Why are we sitting back here in the corner? Did someone offer a little suggestion?"

The marshal was startled. "What the hell do you mean?"

Rocklin shrugged. "Nothing. Forget it."

The marshal lowered his voice and leaned forward, his arms on the table. "I don't like that fishy stare, Rocklin. I don't like you. Get it? I checked up on you, don't think I didn't, but you could be a cattle buyer and still be a Pinkerton. Get out of town, or you're a dead man."

"Well," Rocklin said. "I like to avoid trouble if possible." He eyed the marshal and added, "It interferes with my work as a cattle buyer."

"Leave town, cattle buyer."

"I will. Is the town really split?"

"Right down the middle."

"All right, you gave me some advice . . ."

"I gave you an order."

". . . and now I'll give you some. In a split like that it's always better to be on the right side. Don't be a fool, if you can help it. There's a state senator living right next door, and if he saw some political advantage in it he could get the state's attorney to look into things up here just like that."

Rocklin strolled out of the saloon while Jackson sat and stared after him. He drifted toward the general store and peered into the darkness. The place appeared to be empty. He entered and started browsing among the stacks and shelves, wondering how valuable the business actually was. There seemed to be voices coming from the small office that Mildred Stocker had emerged from in her wheelchair the last time Rocklin was in the store. He walked that way and stopped in the doorway. It was even darker in the office. The voices were louder but still muffled. A small corner of the office was partitioned off and the voices seemed to be coming from there. Then Rocklin saw the stove-pipe hole in the wall above the partition. He heard the loud click of a heavy door, obviously a safe, and ducked back out of the doorway. He was several feet away saying, "Anybody here?" when Mildred Stocker came out of the office, the crutch under one arm. "Oh," he said, "hello, Mrs. Stocker. I was hoping you had gotten in a selection of pipe tobacco."

She grimaced at him and said, "I'm sorry, no. You seem to have stirred up quite a hornet's nest. I'm surprised you're still in town."

"I'll be going soon. The town does seem to be a bit unsettled. Like a different place. But I noticed it when I rode in this morning, some time before Willis cornered me in the restaurant.

"There does seem to be a lot of sudden death for one small place. I mean, not necessarily in the town, but connected with it in one way or another." He laughed. "Well, I'll be watching myself. Good day."

"Good-bye, Mr. Rocklin."

"Oh, I'll be around for a day or two. I have a report to write to Shafter. Your town is becoming known, Mrs. Stocker. I'll be seeing you."

From the store Rocklin walked to the smithy and asked Ollie Winslow if he had time to check a couple of shoes on Buck if he brought him over.

"Be glad to," Winslow said. "Any time."

On his way to the stable, Rocklin stopped by the freight office and found the owner, Con Bracken, unloading a wagon in the adjacent yard. He wished the man a pleasant afternoon and said, "What about you, Mr. Bracken. How do you feel about easier access to a railroad?"

Bracken's tanned face turned sickly gray. He didn't look at Rocklin. His eyes on the ground, he said, "Get out of here. Stay away from me." It was more a plea than a demand, and Rocklin wished the man a good day and moved off. Too bad. It was so simple. Lots of people hated the kind of security they paid Fallon for, but they were afraid of the alternative.

The town seemed quieter in the afternoon sun as Rocklin fetched Buck and rode toward the smithy. He seemed lost in thought, but every nerve was alert. The blacksmith went right to work, lifting each of Buck's hooves and checking the shoe. "The two front ones could be tighter," he said, "but

131

they'll be plenty good for a while longer. I'll fix 'em." Rocklin poked around the neat shop, looking at the variety of well-made tools. He thought there was hardly a thing in the shop except the anvil that Winslow hadn't made himself. He was clearly a master craftsman.

"You're as good as dead, you know," Winslow said in an ordinary tone. He hadn't looked up from his work.

Rocklin continued his inspection. "I can feel it in the air," he admitted.

"Did you hear about the sheriff in Gridley who backed Clayton? Two strangers walked into his office and filled him full of holes." There was no more talk until the blacksmith had finished the job. Rocklin asked him how much and he said two bits. He was feeling around in his pockets for change when he said in the same ordinary tone, "There are those in town who would back someone against Fallon if they thought they had a good enough chance of winning."

Rocklin didn't say anything. When he was mounted he nodded a good-bye and rode off, wondering if he had done the right thing in tipping his hand. It wasn't his usual way of operating, but then it was anything but a usual situation. Besides, he had found out what he needed to know.

CHAPTER 18

His hackles told him something was wrong as he mounted the stairs and walked down the hall to his hotel room, and instinct told him he didn't have a lot of time to decide what to do. Someone was in his room; the signs he had rigged had been disturbed. He decided the best thing would be to walk right in and let them come at him. It was what an ordinary cattle buyer might do. He checked the knife he had concealed on his waist and the doubleaction revolver he always carried in a shoulder holster. He wouldn't use the gun unless he had to, preferring to keep it his secret.

He had the wicked knife in his right hand when he slammed the door open and went in swinging. There was a shot to his left from almost behind the door but he didn't feel anything hit. It flashed through his mind that a man had actually been standing behind the door when it crashed into him and spoiled his shot. He moved swiftly sideways and slammed against the door again, causing another wild shot. A second man was standing facing him, not much more than a yard away. He had been sitting on the bed and had jumped up when Rocklin charged through the door. He snapped off a shot at the doorway, but by that time Rocklin had lunged to the side. With a full swing of his arm, Rocklin laid the man's belly open.

The man behind the door was pushing hard, trying to get free, when Rocklin suddenly released the door. The gunman burst out from behind it as though shot from a cannon, and straight into Rocklin's big hunting knife. He fell against Rocklin, dead weight, and sank to the floor, taking the knife with him flat-bladed between his ribs. He was heavy and was pulling Rocklin off balance so Rocklin let the knife go and turned to the man by the bed. He was staring down at the insides bulging through his shirt. He sat carefully on the bed and wrapped his arms around his middle.

Rocklin stepped to the doorway and yelled, "Hey! Down there! Are you asleep or what? There's a man here who needs a doctor right now. And get the marshal. Damn it, do you hear me!"

The voice of the clerk came. "I hear you. What's going on?"

"What did it sound like, firecrackers? Move!" He was thinking it had been his extreme good luck that the killers had been amateurs.

He didn't give Jackson a chance to say anything as he and two deputies came up the stairs two at a time. "What kind of town are you running here?" he demanded. "I thought the law didn't let hoodlums run around loose. Look at this mess. That man is going to be dead if you don't have someone here in about three minutes to stitch him up."

"What happened?" Jackson asked.

"Can't you see? They were laying for me in my room. Do you think I ran into them in the hall and dragged them in here? Well, what about it, Marshal, I want an explanation." He turned to the clerk, who was hovering just outside the door. "And you'd better have one too, sonny. How did they get in here?"

"This is your fault, Rocklin," Jackson grated. "You stirred this up."

"It's my fault that two gunmen waylaid me and tried to kill me in my room?"

"Look at this," one of the deputies said. He was indicating a ragged bullet hole in the door opposite Rocklin's, a door that was slightly ajar. A man with a black bag hurried up the stairs, but the lawmen were intent on the room. "Jeff," Jackson called, "are you in there?" There was no answer.

"Are you the doctor?" Rocklin asked the man with the black bag.

"And the veterinarian," the man said. "Which do we have here?"

"Men, of a sort," Rocklin said. "One of them is dead and the other is nearly dead, the man on the bed holding himself together."

Jackson was pushing his way in. "I'm in charge here, Rocklin. You shut up." He jerked his head at the other room. "It's old Jeff, Doc. I think he's gone."

"Wild shooting in a hotel. Some law," Rocklin complained. "Who's old Jeff?"

"I said shut up," Jackson yelled.

"Some retired Army man," the doc told Rocklin. "He's lived in that room at least ten years."

"Too bad," Rocklin said. "In a law-abiding town. Well, if I can find my things under this mess I'll find somewhere else to stay. I've had enough of this."

"You're not going anywhere," Jackson said, taking hold of Rocklin's arm.

Rocklin whirled on him and he dropped the arm. "You told me to get out of town and then this happened." Everyone but the doc, who was in Rocklin's room with the patient, stopped to listen. "I can take a hint. Anyone should think twice about standing in my way."

"Where's your gun?" Jackson asked.

"What gun? Do you see a gun?"

"They're both dead now," the doc said, emerging from the room. "Both killed with this knife, I would say." He held up the thing. It wasn't a Bowie but it was a good-size weapon.

"You went in against two men with guns with nothing but this knife?" Jackson asked.

"I didn't know they were there," Rocklin said. "I told you they were laying for me. And the knife is all I happened to have."

"Quite a knife for a cattle buyer," Jackson observed.

"I travel across country, where the cattle are," Rocklin said. "Occasionally I see some kind of

game I would like to have for supper. Excuse me."
He turned away and quickly gathered his belongings and stuffed them in saddlebags. The men in the room watched him in silence, and others, part of a growing crowd in the hall, were peering through when he stopped and turned back to Jackson. "By the way, where's Fallon?"

"Out of town," Jackson said. Then he remembered himself and yelled, "What business is it of yours?"

"Lucky for him," Rocklin said.

"Wait a minute! Have you ever seen these men before?"

"Yes."

"Yes? What do you mean, yes?"

"I saw them in the restaurant this morning. They were wearing deputy badges. You mean you don't know them?"

Jackson was at a loss. Everyone was listening. He stared at Rocklin, grinding his jaw. Finally he blurted, "I don't believe it."

"Ask around. Somebody else must have seen them. Oh, and ask around in Gridley too. I hear a couple of men shot the sheriff to death up there. Better yet, ask Fallon. If you really don't know anything about these killers maybe he does."

CHAPTER 19

Alice Junction was booming. The railroad gang had finished checking the line and was laying a sidetrack for storing cattle cars. The holding pens were almost ready and the saloon, eating place, store, and "hotel," all of them tents, were in full swing. There was a well and a wooden water tank on stilts. It was almost a functioning town, and as well as workers it was drawing cowpokes and curiosity seekers. Some men wore guns and drank too much, but an informal order was imposed by the railroad gang boss and by Hanson Friendly and his hand-picked crew.

There were even some of Fallon's men moving about, taking things in, and Fallon himself rode up one day, sat his horse at a distance and watched the operation. Once a couple of the more sullen protection leaguers tried to start trouble by asking some cowboys from Heismann's spread what they were doing there, but they were quickly surrounded by determined-looking men who strongly suggested they had better git and not come back. They got. Tom Clayton was there, and word had gotten around about Tom Clayton.

Friendly was still enthusiastic about the project, but harboring doubts about Fallon. "I hope it works," he said.

"It will work," Rocklin assured him. "Things in town may come to a boil sooner than we think."

"And what if they don't?" Friendly was looking at Rocklin in a different way since he had heard about the gunmen he had killed with a knife. Some men simply thought it more manly to kill a man with a gun.

"Time is on your side," Rocklin told Friendly. "Let Fallon be the one who gets impatient."

Randy Batcheler, Friendly's youthful foreman, said, "He already is. He's drinking and he's getting meaner."

"Are you in town a lot?" Rocklin asked.

"As often as I can be," Batch said. "I was born there. My folks still live there. Mr. Friendly gave me my first and only job when I was fourteen and I live at the ranch, but Friendly is my hometown. I know everybody in it."

"What are people thinking?" Rocklin asked.

"Well, I'll tell you," Batch said slowly. "They're scared, but more than a few are thinking this might be the time to get rid of Fallon and his gang. If they knew how to do it."

"What else?" Rocklin pressed. "Anything that might be important."

"Well, let's see. The other day Jackson told Fallon he no longer had the right to deputize men, that it was his job, I mean Jackson's. Some say that Fallon put the word out for gunmen. Anyhow, they're drifting in from every hellhole from here to Texas. The word I got is that Fallon was mad enough to kill Jackson. Some say he even threatened to do it."

"Is that so?" Rocklin said. "Interesting."

"Why?" Friendly asked.

"If there's a real battle between Jackson and Fallon . . ." Rocklin paused, searching for a train of thought.

"I was in a corner a lot like this once," Clayton said. "There was a thieving county sheriff on one side and an honest town marshal on the other. It was a matter of picking the right side at the right time."

"Exactly," Rocklin said.

Friendly was nodding thoughtfully. "And, let's see. If we had a chance to . . . if it really came to a break and we had a chance to come down on the side of the real law . . ."

"Could it develop that way in town?" Rocklin asked Batch.

"Seems to me it already is."

"I'll be damned," Friendly said.

"Remember," Rocklin said, "the waiting will be the hardest."

The following Saturday the split between the law officers of Friendly burst apart with a loud crack,

140

and it was Arden Friendly who started the wedge.

Since he was eighteen Batch had been taking Arden Friendly to Saturday night barn dances in town, although he couldn't always get her to go, and lately she hadn't wanted to go much at all. But he was the best dancer among the men and she was good, very good when she was able to relax. Also, Batch, with his unfailing good humor and goodwill, was popular in town, with men as well as women.

When they decided to ride into town early that Saturday afternoon and stay for the dance, Rocklin and Clayton decided to go along, Rocklin because Friendly had indicated that he would feel better about it, and Clayton because he wanted to keep an eye on Arden, who, he was well aware, was playing a game with him and Batch.

Batch was aware of the game too and, exactly like Clayton, was amused and indulgent. He knew that Clayton was in love with Arden, just as he had been for as long as he could remember, but he also knew that Arden was not ready to love anybody and that it might be a long time before she was. He would wait. But would Clayton?

Arden was leading them into town from the east across the plain, riding ahead with Rocklin and talking animatedly about the Brontë sisters, Shakespeare, and the merits of Helen Hunt Jackson's novel *Ramona*.

The town was alive with people; people sitting on the grass of the square, or milling about the streets, or crowding the saloon, restaurant, and store. Strangely, there wasn't much talk, except in undertones, and there were sidelong glances and a wide berth for the men wearing guns.

"I've never seen anything like it," Batch said as they dismounted in front of the store. "What's going on?"

"It's exciting," Arden said, "but it's . . . it's scary. Do you know what it reminds me of, Batch? It's like the eerie atmosphere that day just before that awful storm hit. What is it, Mr. Rocklin?"

"I agree with you, Miss Friendly. A storm warning. 'There is something in the wind.' "

She laughed with delight and took his arm. "A nemesis who quotes Shakespeare," she said. "Wonderful."

"I think it might be better if we took Miss Friendly home." Tom Clayton said.

"He's right, Arden," Batch said.

"He certainly is," Rocklin agreed.

"Oh, pooh. You men always hog all the fun. I'm staying. I want to start out with some pie and coffee. Mrs. Richards cooks all the pies for the hotel, and her gooseberry is something special. I know because Jancie Richards was my best friend when I was a kid and I stayed overnight with her lots of times."

"You're not friends anymore?" Rocklin asked.

"No. She left town. She just disappeared one day. I cried for a week."

"Your father mentioned a girl who disappeared,"

Rocklin said.

"That was Jancie. Personally, I think someone kidnapped her and sold her to a white slave ring." Clayton looked at her with amusement, Batch turned red and looked as though he would like to turn her over his knee and Rocklin looked interested and said, "Do you really?"

"Oh, I don't know," Arden told him. "There was talk. Some of the men in this town do anything they feel like doing and there's nobody to stop them. I wouldn't put anything past that Fallon."

"Did someone mention my name?" Fallon growled. He had stepped out of the hotel lobby just after the four had passed and was directly behind them on the walk. Batch and Arden were facing him when they turned around. Clayton and Rocklin moved toward Fallon, but two gunmen had followed Fallon out of the hotel and were watching, hands on six-shooters. Rocklin was armed, but his weapons were well concealed. "You know, Miss Friendly," Fallon sneered, "you've been calling me a murderer for too long. You're going to find yourself in jail if you don't learn to keep your silly mouth shut."

Batch hit him in the mouth and knocked him down. Clayton moved fast but found himself looking at a Colt .45 about an inch from his nose. The other man waved his gun in the general direction of Rocklin.

"All right," Fallon told his gunmen as he came off the ground. "He's all mine." He looked at

143

Clayton. "I'll get to you next, big shot."

Clayton laughed at him. "Don't be too sure," he said.

The ex-marshal was two inches taller and fifty pounds heavier than Batch, but booze, laziness, and hate had taken their toll. He didn't know it yet, but the day he could kill any man with his fists was gone. First he would have to hit him, and Batch was as tough and quick as a bullwhip.

Rocklin edged toward Arden and said, "Walk casually to your horse, get on it, and go home." There was a gleam in her eye and she thought she was going to argue. "Now," Rocklin ordered quietly. She glared at him but turned and started down the walk. The gunman who was more or less covering Rocklin moved to intercept her but was too uncertain about it. Rocklin moved between them and said, "Quickly!" She left.

Fallon had tried three times to hit Batch and had been punched three times in the mouth, all the blows landing in exactly the same place. He gave it up and came at the smaller man like an enraged bear.

"Ten to five that your boss loses," Rocklin told the astonished gunman.

"Fallon will kill him if he can ever get hold of him," the man replied. "Oh-oh. It's over now."

Everyone in town had gathered to watch the fight and they were crowding too close. Batch had less and less room to maneuver, and finally Fallon caught his fist and whirled him around. Now Fallon had both fists, one locked around a wrist for leverage, grinding into Batch's solar plexus. Batch writhed and flailed, but Fallon just lifted him off the ground and kept squeezing. Batch tried rolling backward but he wasn't tall enough to get any purchase on the ground. He tried reaching back and pounding on Fallon's ribs with both fists. He tried a forward roll in an effort to throw Fallon head-on into a building. He was not easy to kill, and Fallon was tiring, breathing hard.

There was a pause in the death struggle. Fallon was almost exhausted and wanted to try for a fresh lock on his victim. Batch was beginning to see black. Then he felt Fallon's grip loosen and shift slightly. He took a quick gulp of air and slid down an inch, feeling solid ground under his feet for the first time since Fallon wrapped him up. He tightened his muscles and struggled harder. Fallon wanted to end it; he knew he couldn't keep the pressure on much longer. He bore down with all his strength. Batch's face was turning purple and he knew it was just about over. He went limp, as though losing consciousness, felt his heel next to Fallon's foot, lifted it and came down hard. Fallon's grip loosened and he fell to the ground, taking Batch with him. Batch rolled quickly away and lay there taking in great swallows of air. There was a strange sound from the crowd, like a great sigh that was part moan.

Fallon was struggling to get up and Jackson came to him and lifted. The man was standing on one foot, balancing on the heel of the other, not yet feeling the real pain. He stared at Batch with intense hatred, ran his hand across his mouth and stared at the blood on it. Then he put his hand on his gun. The crowd backed up.

"Don't be a fool, Fallon," Jackson warned.

"Stay out of it," Fallon growled, but he let go of the gun. "Take him," he said to his men.

"Wait," Jackson urged.

"Shut up. You heard me," he told his men. "Take him. He attacked an officer of the law."

The group moved toward the jail and the crowd followed. The man covering Clayton prodded him along with the point of his gun.

"You owe me five dollars," Rocklin told the gunman tagging along beside him.

The man grinned. "Try to collect," he said.

"Not to the jail," Fallon told his men. "Take him to the stable." The crowd, increasingly disturbed, followed along making disapproving sounds. "Get a buggy whip," Fallon told the stable owner as they approached the big double door.

"What for?" the owner demanded.

Fallon drew his gun. "Get it." The man turned into the stable and Fallon told his gunmen, "Nail his hands to the door." There were angry protests from the crowd and Fallon turned his gun toward it. "If anybody sticks his nose in, lock him up. Red. Dick. Go inside and get a hammer and some nails and do as I tell you." Red and Dick didn't move. They looked at Jackson.

Rocklin sidled toward Jackson; his guard followed with gun in hand but not pointed. "This is your chance, Jackson," Rocklin said. "If you want to be the top man in town, use your head." Jackson didn't move. Rocklin edged closer to Clayton and the man holding a gun to his back.

"All right," Fallon yelled. "All the men who are with me. You men I just hired. Take your guns out." Half a dozen men drew guns. "Now go inside and get a hammer and nails and get on with it." Someone in the crowd said, "Rush 'em," and Fallon ordered, "Shoot anyone who moves."

Four men wrestled Batch to the stable door and another started pounding a nail through his left hand. Rocklin's guard was intent on the torture and didn't see the knife and the swift movement that slashed the wrist of his gun hand to the bone. The man with the gun in Clayton's back was suddenly aware that the muzzle of a revolver was poking steadily at the corner of his right eye.

The instant Clayton felt the pressure on his back ease and heard the gun fall to the ground, he moved forward like a panther and slid Fallon's gun from its holster.

"All right," he shouted. "Everybody hold it and take a good look." Four guns pointed his way. "I said take a good look," he repeated. He had the muzzle of the gun sticking in Fallon's ear. The trigger was pulled all the way back and his thumb was hooked over the fully cocked hammer. "If anyone so much as breathes on me, Fallon is going to have his brains blown out. Do you understand, Fallon?" The ex-marshal was silent. "Say it," Clayton demanded.

"I understand," Fallon muttered. He was beginning to feel the pain in his foot and his battered mouth.

"Tell them to put their guns on the ground."

"Put your guns down," Fallon said.

Jackson came alive. "All right," he shouted, "all the men who had anything to do with this are no longer deputies. I'm the marshal of this town"—there was some snickering from the crowd—"and you are all fired. Including you, Fallon."

Fallon sneered at him. "I still run the protective league, remember."

"But you have no standing as a lawman, as of now. You will no longer wear a gun in this town."

"We'll see," Fallon said. He turned to Clayton. "And I'll see you outside of town. Have a gun."

The doc went to Batch and looked at his hand. "I'd better cauterize that right now," he said. "A stable is no place to get a puncture wound. I've seen a man die of lockjaw."

"So have I," Batch said.

As the crowd thinned, Rocklin turned and saw Mildred Stocker watching him from the back door of her store. He stared back at her for a moment and then he and Clayton started to move away.

"Heading back?" Clayton asked.

"A little later," Rocklin replied. "I want to talk to a couple of the farmers before they go home."

"I'll see you, then. I'm going to check on Batch and then leave. I've had enough of this place for one day."

"I'll go with you. I've got an idea."

"Oh-oh."

There were people standing around the front of the doctor's neat frame house in back of the school. They were talking about the incident and they were angry.

The doctor had opened the nail hole in Batch's hand with a thin surgical knife so it would bleed freely and had washed it thoroughly with a syringe and carbolic acid solution. Batch was looking pale but ready to go.

"Whatever you do," Rocklin said, "try to stop your boss from riding into town after Fallon."

"I'm going after Fallon," Randy said.

"No. Fallon is through. All he needs is a little more rope. Sit tight."

"I can't. And Friendly won't. Fallon insulted his daughter. You ought to understand that, Rocklin."

"I don't think anyone could stop me in your place," Clayton said, "but I believe Rocklin is right. It's practically all over. It'll take more nerve to wait. Also a cool head." He turned to Rocklin. "You said you had an idea."

"I was wondering if Friendly could arrange a party, a sort of town-warming for tomorrow at the junction. The place is ready for it. Do you think there would be enough time to get the word around?"

149

Clayton laughed. "A real sneaky idea, Rocklin. Just at the right time too."

Batch was considering. "I don't see why he couldn't do it. We have enough men to pass the word all over the county this afternoon. I could get a lot of help here in town right now. He'll say it would be better if he had more time, though."

"I have a feeling this is the time," Rocklin said.

"It sure looks like it," Batch agreed. "The whole town of Friendly might drift over to see Alice Junction. After church, I mean."

Batch's friends crowded around as he left the doctor's place and he drew several of them aside and talked to them briefly. They nodded in quick understanding and went their way.

When the three men had mounted and Batch and Clayton were about to veer off toward the ranch, Clayton said to Rocklin, "By the way, did you notice what was going on at Mildred Stocker's storage shed when we were heading for the stable?"

Rocklin nodded. "Unloading dynamite from one of Con Bracken's wagons."

"A lot of dynamite for one small cattle and farming town."

"I wonder what's going on in that twisted mind," Rocklin said.

CHAPTER 20

What was going on in Mildred Stocker's twisted mind at that moment was the problem of Jack Fallon. She was trying to decide whether to kill him outright or arrange some trap that would accomplish the same thing and leave her in the clear. She had decided on the latter and was thinking of a way to do it when the would-be victim slipped through the back door of the store and approached the office.

"Sit down," she said. "I was just trying to think of a way out of the mess your stupidity has created."

Fallon sat. He stared into the hated eyes for a minute and suddenly drew his gun and pointed it at her throat. "It would be a pleasure to blast a hole right in your scrawny neck," he told her.

"But not now," she said. "You would hang. Besides, I have my finger on the triggers of a sawed-off shotgun that would cut you in two. You'll just have to wait." She leaned back in her wheelchair but she didn't take her hands from under the blanket in her lap. "You've completely lost control, Fallon, so the only question is, what good are you. Can you think of a way to get it back?"

"Maybe."

"Well what is it," she snapped.

"Don't wait. Raid the rail town right away . . ."

"They'll be waiting for you. We've gone over all that . . ."

"Wait a minute, dammit. At the same time we draw them into this town."

"How?"

"By grabbing Arden Friendly."

The woman smiled in a grotesque way. "You would like that, wouldn't you? And would you kill her the way you killed the Richards child? Wonderful."

Fallon drew his gun again. This time he pointed it at her nose, almost touching it, and he cocked it. "Do you want to hear this?"

"Go on. But if you point that gun once more, pull the trigger. Because I will."

"You don't care if you die, you crazy old woman."

"You should keep that in mind. Go on."

"What I do with the girl will be none of your business. I'll draw Friendly's men away from the junction and my men will burn it or blow it up. You'll give me fifty thousand dollars and you'll never see me again. You'll be in the clear." He laughed in an ugly way. "You won't want to see me again because I'll be on the run anyway, so you'll have nothing to hold over my head. And I'll have nothing to lose by shooting you to rags."

They stared at each other again and finally Fallon demanded, "Well?"

"All right," she said, "but on one condition. Take ten thousand more, get into Flack's shop and plant it there, kill Flack and ransack the place. Then take your girl and don't come back. You won't anyway. You'll be hanging from a tree within a week."

He tensed. "Because you'll talk."

"I won't have to, you fool. You'll have Friendly and Clayton and Rocklin after you, with all the men they can muster, before you get out of the township. Arden Friendly isn't some poor farm girl. And, by the way, what about Rocklin?"

"What about him?"

"I'm losing patience with you." The flat tone of the statement and the expressionless stare lifted the hairs on the back of the crude man's neck. He was afraid of the woman but he could never admit or even realize it. He could only get violently angry, which left him weaker and more muddled. "What's this bee in your bonnet about Rocklin? I've told you, Jackson checked on him and I checked on him. He's buying cattle for Shafter. The head of the company vouched for him. Twice."

"Twice was a mistake. After the first time the head of the company would surely let him know that questions were being asked. Can't I leave anything to you? Why is he still around here?"

"He's seeing a lot of people. Even some pig farmers and anyone with a few sheep. Forget him. He's a buyer."

She shook her head at him in disgust. "A buyer. Before he even got into town he knocked Gasser Mann cold. Then, cool as you please, he stepped in to stop you from starting a gun battle in the middle of a crowd. Then Gasser" — she made one of her grimaces at the name — "went out to Three Rocks to lay for him and ended up dead.

"Then he talked Hanson Friendly into starting the rail town . . . save the arguments; I know he did it. Hanson Friendly would never think of that by himself. *Then* he talked Clay Washington Major into the project when Major had sworn he would see the town of Friendly rot on the vine. *Then,* when I told you to hire a couple of men to get the drop on him and take him out on the prairie and kill him, *you* hire a couple of morons who sit and wait for *him* to surprise *them* . . ."

"You don't know that for sure."

" . . . after *you* pinned deputy badges on them and let them wander around town. And certainly I know that. He walked into the room with his knife in his hand, otherwise it could never have happened the way it did. *Then* he almost cuts a hand off a man who has a gun on him, disarms another man . . ."

"Everybody was watching . . ."

"Yes. Everybody was watching your latest bit of

154

idiocy. And Rocklin waited for just that moment . . ."

"He's *not* a Pinkerton. We checked."

"Whatever he is, he's working for Friendly. And with your help *he's destroying everything I built.*"

"If what you say is true, he's after *me*. He doesn't even know who you are."

"He knows."

Fallon sat for a long moment staring at a wall. He felt his swollen and livid mouth. "All right. I'll burn down Friendly's damn rail town and I'll leave the girl alone. I'll grab Batcheler. That'll draw them in."

"And don't forget to plant the money in Flack's place and kill him. Make it look good."

His grin had a sneer in it. "Then all you have to do is see that Jackson is tipped off in some way so I'm killed coming out of the shop and you're home free."

She reminded herself again that the man, although not very intelligent, was cunning. "That's an idea. But now that you've thought of it you can easily avoid it—the trap, I mean—and you can tell anyone at any time that I was the one who set up the whole protection system."

"Not if I'm dead. Well, to hell with it." He got up. "I'll let you know." He turned and walked out of the office.

Mildred Stocker sat awhile in thought, then rolled through the store to the front walk. Her husband was there sweeping. People were leaving town. They were in a far different mood than they had been earlier in the day.

"Is Rocklin still in town, Newton?" He shook his head once without stopping his sweeping. She sat in her chair on the walk, watching the comings and goings. She had the thought that everyone was deserting the town, deserting her, and she hated them all.

Rocklin walked out of the hotel, looked around, saw her, and started toward her. She put on her grimace of a smile and said, "Mr. Rocklin. There you are. I got in some of that tobacco you wanted."

"Good," Rocklin said. He followed her into the store and during the transaction they exchanged pleasantries.

"I regret very much that terrible trouble in your room. If you find it convenient you may stay in the hotel as long as you wish, without charge," she told him.

"That's very good of you. I may take advantage of your offer. I'm not quite finished here yet."

"I hope your visit has been successful," she said, rolling toward her office in an invitation for him to follow.

"Just a few loose ends," he said.

"Come in, come in. Sit down. We haven't really had a chance to talk at all. Tell me, what do you think of our town?" She was gazing at him with what she thought was a frank and open countenance. She had seldom looked more malevolent.

"It's hard to assess in a short visit." He took a seat across from her at the desk.

"And does your employer expect you to assess the communities where he does business?"

"To some extent, yes. The packing plant is going to need a steady and dependable supply source. It's up to me to advise the owners whether they can expect that."

She smiled her crooked smile. "And do you go so far as to bring order to a community so you can have a dependable supply?"

He grinned back at her, "I do what I can."

"I see. Without disturbing the peace of the community, of course."

"Of course. Although I must say that from the time I came to the first roadblock at the town of Friendly I haven't seen much peace."

She nodded. "I'm afraid that's true. I suppose you just came at a bad time. Have you ever been a lawman, Mr. Rocklin?"

"Never."

"Too bad. You seem most capable." She let it hang and Rocklin was not inclined to help her any. The dim light in the office was growing dimmer and the woman stretched the silence by lighting a kerosene lamp. It didn't help much; the lamp's chimney was streaked with black. In the silence Rocklin could clearly hear the sound of a poker game coming through the stovepipe hole high in the wall back of her chair. She was looking at him as he glanced up at the hole. She grinned again.

Rocklin noticed that her teeth were good. In fact, her features would be attractive in a straight forward way if her face was ever in repose. He wondered, not for the first time, why tragedy twists some people for life and seems to strengthen others.

"Yes," she said. "I can know everything of importance going on in town, just by sitting here and listening."

"That's why the marshal makes that corner his unofficial office. Does the acting marshal know why he sits there?"

"No, and he never will. He's not the man for the job." She paused. "But you could be."

Although it didn't show, Rocklin was so surprised that he decided to stall. He was surprised in two ways: that she would misjudge him so badly in offering so blatant a bribe and that she would be so careless as to reveal to him how desperate she was.

After a whole minute had ticked away he asked, "Are you speaking for the town council or is this your own idea?"

"Oh, let's not put a friendly talk on an official basis. You understand that as marshal you would also be head of the Citizens Protective League."

"I see. And what would my share of the take be?"

She smiled again, but this time with a new twist. He couldn't read it at first, then it struck him that there was a certain glee in the strange smile. She was pleased with herself. Apparently she had just gotten another confirmation of her opinion of men, all men.

"Twenty percent."

"Meaning?"

"About twenty thousand dollars a year."

"From this little corner of the state? I don't believe it."

"I can show you figures. The cattle alone . . . but we're going too fast. Are you saying you'll do it?"

"Not for twenty percent. But what if I could buy into the business for a reasonable sum, say, fifty thousand? Could we make it an even split? After all, I'll be taking all the risks."

"And I'll be providing the enterprise," she snapped. "You can't expect to get back your investment the first year."

"Well, we should be able to work it out. It's essential, wouldn't you say, that we start out right together, on an amicable basis, I mean."

"By all means."

"Give me a chance to think it over. The business does seem to be, uh, in danger of falling apart."

"That's where you come in."

"All right. Let's see if we can work out an acceptable partnership deal. I'll be talking to you later. Oh, and I'm not Fallon. I haven't murdered a farm girl. You won't have a spade bit to jerk me around with."

Now it was Mildred's turn to control her surprise

before she spoke. Her stare was all the more threatening because of its blankness. Rocklin became very aware that her hands were out of sight under the robe in her lap. She laughed. It sounded as though she was choking for breath.

"I didn't have one on Fallon. He just thought I did."

"And he had killed the girl before Friendly brought him in."

She nodded. "He was still sheriff in Gridley. Someone had seen him with the girl, someone who is now dead. I made a guess and told him he had been seen when he buried her out in the plain. His cowardice made that enough."

All of it past tense, Rocklin thought. Jack Fallon had been written off. Which made him all the more dangerous.

"I'll talk to you later, then."

CHAPTER 21

The people started drifting in long before noon. Some of them Hanson Friendly had never seen before, hardy souls originally from back East and even a lot farther than that, from Germany and Scandinavia and Holland, some of whom could speak little English; pig farmers, dairy farmers, corn farmers, wheat farmers, mostly from the extreme east end of the broad county where the grass was a little higher and the climate a little wetter, venture some folks lured by the promise of cheap land who were eager to take risks for freedom and for profit, many of whom had never seen a trail town and wanted to find out what it was all about.

What they saw was fairly typical; no frame buildings so far, but a number of tent structures with wood floors that made up the "business" section; families who had decided to try their luck in the new town living in tents, and not even tents of canvas or animal hide but of old blankets and muslin sheets; two or three families who had found sites on slight rises, had dug cavelike holes in the sides of the rises and covered the holes with roofs of sod laced with tough and tangled roots of grass, a "soddie," a place to call home, maybe for years, until the owners could make enough money to buy expensive lumber, every board-foot of which would have to be freighted in, and meanwhile they would be cozy enough in their soddies, warmer in winter, cooler in summer and a lot safer than they would be in a frame house when a grass fire roared down on them like a tornado.

Folks from the towns of Friendly and Gridley came a little later, and they were astonished at what had been accomplished at Alice Junction in so short a time.

Rocklin, who hadn't been at the site for almost a week, was astonished too. A windmill was up, and pumping heartily in the brisk wind. The railroad gang had finished their work and left, but Rocklin reckoned that the town's more or less permanent population might still be as much as thirty or forty. He wondered how they were going to survive until the herds started coming and made a mental note to check with Shafter and see how soon some feeding pens would be ready. Maybe he could hurry them up.

But for the growing crowd it was not a day for worrying. The people had come for food, recreation, excitement, and to get acquainted. Some of the women had left their poke bonnets and gingham at home and sported their Sunday clothes; the men too. Even most of the cowboys were in their Sunday best, a few of them swaggering around with guns on their hips making bold overtures to the teenage farm girls, most of whom were shyly willing but most of whose parents were sternly watchful. The cowboys were too free, too often far from home, and who knew what went on in towns just like this one at the end of a long cattle drive, even if they often were quite young, quite reticent, and quite respectful of womenfolk. Yes, there was the devil-may-care bunch too, with their guns and occasionally with guitars or banjos slung over their shoulders, romantic figures to the girls.

Two or three of the watchful fathers had brought along fiddles, and there were two concertinas, several harmonicas, and even a trumpet. After dinner there would be dancing and, inevitably, several weeks or months hence a farm girl or two would announce that she wanted to get married to some cowboy from such-and-such ranch, demonstrating that the young people had managed, as usual—the parents all unaware, as usual—and more often than not the girl had kept her virtue and, incidentally, the boy his honor. There were community sanctions for those who did not, and although those sanctions could be bad for the youngsters, they were good for the community in the long run.

Rocklin was taking it all in when he became aware of a developing scene at the western trail-end of the town. Four riders wearing badges were confronting three men standing in the road. He strolled that way to find Hanson Friendly saying, "I said you were welcome and you are. But you'll take off your badges and your guns or you'll leave."

"Other men are wearing guns," one of the four said. "But you men aren't. How are you going to make us?"

Tom Clayton and Randy Batcheler took a step toward the men and stopped. The men tensed in their saddles and the spokesman put his hand on his gun. Batcheler's expression, like Friendly's, was impassive, but Clayton had a funny kind of smile.

"Other men are not part of Fallon's gang," Friendly said, "and I don't think we'll have to make you. This is a social. What's it going to be?"

His calm and almost affable tone caused the four men to glance around. All they saw were people enjoying themselves. Then Rocklin strolled up. They looked at him. Then they looked at Clayton, then at Friendly and Batch. "I should mention that if you do stay," Friendly said, "it wouldn't be polite to take down names for Fallon, or anything like that." The men glanced around again, then they took a good look at the men blocking their way. They turned their horses and left. But they hung around the far fringes of the town the rest of the day. When they reported, Fallon—and Mildred Stocker—would have a good clear idea of the threat posed by Alice Junction.

Hanson Friendly looked around and wondered, not for the first time, where they had all come from. "I thought I knew just about everybody in these parts," he said. "And how did they all get word?"

Arden joined them. "Batch has a lot of friends," she said, taking his arm. She had been concerned for her longtime friend and had stuck fairly close to him since his return from town the day before. She hadn't been told what had happened to his hand but had pieced the story together from what she had heard at the social, and she had her own idea about what to do to Jack Fallon.

"I've talked to some of them," Rocklin said, "and do you know what? A bunch of them from east county had already planned to come and see the new town and make a day of it."

"They must have started before dawn," Friendly said.

"And traveled the better part of eight hours," Rocklin said. "Some of them tell me they plan to stay overnight and start back at dawn tomorrow. They can't believe they were met by a celebration."

Hanson Friendly chuckled. "It's a good thing I had the men put a few head of beef in the pens. I wanted to make the place look busy; now I may have to butcher a couple more of them." He was having a good time.

One of the reasons the day was going so well was Alice Friendly's homely grace. She was everywhere, fascinated by the scene, and no one she met was a stranger. Before the day was half over, people were talking about Alice Friendly, and every time her husband took her arm he beamed.

When the food came there wasn't much variety

but there was plenty of it. Lots of steak, three cast iron pots holding ten gallons of chili each and simmering over open fires, corn bread and wheat bread, potato salad and pickled beets and watermelon pickles and berry pies brought by the farm women — who hadn't expected a blowout — and shared with the crowd while it lasted. Folks gathered in more intimate groups when it came time to eat, using tables from the tent restaurant, or the tailgates of wagons, or merely spreading a blanket on a patch of grass.

But during the games and the later dancing it was a free-for-all — gunny-sack races, foot races, horse races, plain wrestling and Indian wrestling, shooting exhibitions using rocks and a couple of old tin cans, riding and roping shows, the last, astonishing some of the recently settled farmers who had never seen a cowhand snag a running steer by a hind leg with a seventy-foot rope and dump it neatly in the dirt, and who thought it the most skillful bit of sleight-of-hand they had ever witnessed.

There were surprisingly few sore-head losers from the contests and they were quickly laughed out of their tempers by the cheerful crowd. There was an openness about the whole scene that made pretense difficult and revealed a great deal about individual character and temperament.

The dancing, on the cleared floor of the restaurant, was spirited and fun. Some of the young men might take an intense dislike for a competitor, but it was usually momentary — and usually apparent to

166

anyone watching. The celebrants tacitly drew the lines, and if anyone crossed them who couldn't be kidded into behaving he was taken aside by a few older men and told which cow ate the cabbage.

Arden Friendly was much in demand. She was a competent dancer and she had prudently decided to leave any stylish eastern outfit at home and wear a simple western skirt of ankle length, blouse with a little lace at the neck, and a jacket of soft suede with a bit of embroidery. She stood out, all right, but not forbiddingly so. She favored Batch most of the evening, until Clayton wondered, without much amusement, if she was doing it on purpose. When she and Batch were about to go into their third dance in a row, Clayton slipped between them, said laughingly to Batch, "Oh no you don't," and led her outside.

They were standing alone at a corner of the fence. The cows had started to wander to the far side of the pens at their approach and they could hear the faint movement beneath the talk and laughter of the dance floor. The musicians had stopped for a rest, and the sound of people enjoying themselves, the shuffling of life in the pens and ceaseless movement of the grass only made the vast silence of the world and the sky, high wispy clouds slipping by a sliver of a moon, more intense. Their heartbeats seemed loud in their ears. He kissed her and she kissed him back and the kiss was part of the night and the silence. She rested her forehead on his chest for a moment and for both of them the feeling of holding someone was marvelous beyond words. They were young and they wondered why it wasn't possible to hold each other forever.

The music started, and the stomping. They stood slightly apart, aware of the darkness and of their thoughts. They stayed that way for a long time without uttering a sound, they kissed again, a quicker, harder one this time, and started walking.

"Is it much different in Texas?" she asked.

"Quite a bit," he said, ignoring her meaning. "We have trees, different terrain, different grass. The moon's the same."

She laughed at him softly and he thought it the most enchanting sound he had ever heard. "How old are you, Tom Clayton?" she asked.

"That's good," he said. "Mix reality with romance. I'm thirty."

"And how is it that you have never married?"

"I don't know. I guess the right girl hasn't come along."

She laughed again, wholly aware of how it charmed him. "And of course you have very definite ideas about that right girl?"

He thought for a minute and said, "No. Not very definite, just vaguely definite."

"Ah. Good!" The paradox delighted her. "And of course you would never ask a girl to marry you just because you were passionately in love."

"And trust to luck? I don't know. Would you?"

"I would meet him on the street, or on a train, or he would ride one day into the ranch. He would look at me and say, 'Come.' And he would reach down and pull me up to the back of his saddle and

I wouldn't look back."

It was Clayton's turn to laugh at her, and she had the sense of humor to laugh with him. He said, "I've thought of asking you to marry me . . ."

"How thrilling!"

" . . . but I'm afraid you'd say yes and no." They laughed some more.

"What about Batch?" he asked, taking a chance.

"To him I would say no and yes." This time there was less humor in the laughter. The magic was wispier than the clouds.

"Well," he said, "if you ever reach the point where you are of one mind . . ."

"Yes. That would be necessary, wouldn't it."

"She was trying to find out how much you know," Clayton suggested.

The party had quieted down, although there were still those who would dance until the musicians dropped of exhaustion, and the four men had taken the opportunity to talk privately. Rocklin had told them of the development in town and they were puzzling over it.

"I don't think so," Rocklin said. "It seemed to me that she deliberately made it plain that she knew I knew."

"Mildred Stocker," Friendly said. "I just can't believe it. You're sure there's not . . ." He let the thought dwindle away.

"Then you're probably right," Clayton said to Rocklin. "It was just a last desperate maneuver."

"It looks that way. I hope so."

"What worries me . . ." It was Friendly who spoke. They all looked at him. "I wonder if they would hit us tonight."

"Oh." Rocklin thought it over. "It doesn't seem . . ."

"Batch?" Friendly inquired.

The foreman considered. "Not very likely, I'd say. They know the situation here. They wouldn't risk being seen by too many people. Anyhow, I'll have men posted all along the trail all night. If anyone starts this way we'll find out about it right quick."

"I don't think Fallon will wait long, though," Clayton said.

"Tomorrow night is my guess," Rocklin agreed.

Friendly turned to Batch. "Have a couple of men keep track of Arden. I don't want her going near town."

CHAPTER 22

The next day Arden Friendly talked the two cowhands who were following her everywhere into riding into town with her for just a minute, and Jack Fallon arrested her for carrying a gun.

The news was brought to Hanson Friendly by one of the cowhands, who had ridden from the town to the ranch with a bullet in his gut and who died minutes later.

Fallon, who had long been aware that Arden Friendly sometimes carried a derringer in an inside pocket of her riding jacket, and who hadn't forgotten that the girl had undoubtedly shot him once before, couldn't resist the chance when he spotted the telltale sag in the jacket.

Arden and her escorts had barely dismounted when Fallon confronted her and said he would take the derringer. She challenged him to just try it and he did. In the brief scuffle one of Arden's unarmed guardians was shot and the other cold-cocked. Three of Fallon's gunmen dragged the girl and the unconscious man off to jail, leaving the wounded man lying in the street. Most of the onlookers followed the procession to the jail, many of them protesting all the way. A couple of them tried to help the wounded man, but he dragged himself to his horse and made a beeline to the ranch.

He died before he could give a clear account of what had happened, but when Rocklin and Clayton rode into the ranch from Alice Junction, where they had seen the overnight guests on their way, Friendly and Batch and twenty heavily armed Circle H men were ready to ride into town and take Arden out of jail, even if they had to reduce the town to splinters.

Rocklin wanted to know what was happening, but all he got from Friendly was "Stay out of this, Rocklin," and Batch filled him in as best he could.

"Wait a minute," Rocklin urged.

"I said stay out," Friendly ordered. "Come on, Batch . . ."

Rocklin pulled the double-action .38 from under his arm and shot three times in the air. It got their attention.

Friendly was seeing red. "Rocklin," he said in a menacing voice, "if you try to interfere again . . ."

"Shut up," Rocklin said. It was like a whip crack. Hanson Friendly was momentarily shocked speechless. No one had spoken to him like that since he was a boy. "You've got Fallon licked, you fool. Don't you see that?" The shock tactics worked. Friendly shook his head like a horse being worried by an incompetent rider. "Are you going to throw it all in now?"

"Do you know what you're talking about," Friendly demanded. "What would you do? Sneak up on him in the dark with a knife?"

Rocklin understood the insult and ignored it. "I sure as hell wouldn't ride into Friendly with two dozen men, putting myself in the wrong with the law and leaving Alice Junction wide open to an attack."

"Damn Alice Junction! He's got my daughter in jail!"

"Where she'll be out of trouble and out of the way. At least for a while." For a second Rocklin thought the man was going to shoot him, but something happened. Everybody saw it; a gleam of intelligence returned to his eyes.

"You don't know that Fallon will hit the junction tonight. You're gambling, and you're using my daughter as the stake. What kind of man are you?"

"Think, Mr. Friendly. This is exactly what Fallon's been waiting for. He's just sitting there with his mouth watering, waiting for you to storm the place with a war party like this. Hell, this is his last chance, and you're going to give it to him."

"He can't have figured this. He's not that smart," Friendly argued.

"He didn't have to figure. It fell into his lap."

Batch was staring thoughtfully at his boss and

the men were shifting in their saddles. There was a pause and a turning point. "All right, I'm listening," Friendly growled. "What's your idea?"

"Go into town by yourself . . ."

"I'll ride with him," Clayton said.

"No. Fallon hates you. It will just make him crazier. Batch can go. He has friends and he has the sympathy of the town. And don't forget, Fallon killed an unarmed man who was only trying to protect a woman."

"And then what?" Friendly asked.

"Follow the rules. See Jackson. See the mayor. Talk to the councilmen. Don't argue the case, just insist on bail. Drag it out. Make Fallon think just what you said—damn Alice Junction as long as your daughter is in jail. Is everything set up there?"

"Yes. I'll send a man to alert the posse in Gridley. They sent a federal marshal in there after the sheriff was killed, and the junction is mostly in his territory. I know him, and he's dependable.

"But there's just one thing, Rocklin. You admit that Fallon has gone loco. What if he's loco enough to go against Jackson and take over the town while he's holding my daughter?"

"Then," Rocklin said, "you have a good chance of taking it over yourself, with the town's backing and maybe even with Jackson's help. Remember what we talked about?"

"And if my daughter gets killed?"

"I don't think she will."

"But there's no guarantee," Friendly insisted.

"You know there isn't. But this is our best chance. You have the final say-so. Think it over."

"What do you think, Batch?" Friendly asked.

"It sounds right. I can't think of anything better."

"What about you, Clayton? I mean, what's your opinion. You don't have to get involved."

"I am involved. But I think we could use four or five men, if they rode in one at a time and if we spotted them out of sight. Somewhere that would give them a good clear shot at the jail." He added, "If that became necessary.

"One man might even go up the water tower and tell the lookout that Jackson sent him. Pick the best men you've got with a rifle."

Friendly and Batcheler had plenty of time to get the whole county on their side as they went from person to person and from place to place, getting entangled in indecision, procrastination, and buck passing—while time ran out.

When they asked to see Arden, Jackson put them off, saying it wasn't a good time. He assured them she was fine and so was the man with her, and asked if they would mind coming back later in the afternoon. Friendly, holding his temper, asked why he couldn't just pay the usual fine for carrying a gun and take her home.

Jackson seemed out of his depth and a little embarrassed. "Well, it's not as simple as that, Mr. Friendly."

"Why not?"

"Well, there's a charge of striking a law officer, and interfering with an officer and resisting arrest. . ."

"What officer?" Batch asked.

"Well, Fallon."

"I heard you fire him; the whole town did," Batch said. "And you told him he couldn't carry a gun in town anymore. The next thing you know he kills a man and locks a woman in the jail. What are you doing about that?"

"Well, I guess I was a little too previous. Some of the councilmen, a couple anyway, seemed to think I was. Look, just give me a little time and I'll get it straightened out . . ."

"You don't have much time," Friendly threatened. "You . . ."

"Mr. Friendly," Batch interrupted, "I think we ought to go see Mr. Willis."

Jackson seized on the suggestion. "That would be your best bet, Mr. Friendly. It really would. And I'll talk to . . . I'll see what I can do."

The mayor's contribution was "An awful thing to happen. A terrible thing. We're going to get to the bottom of it, Hanson, I promise you. I've called a meeting of the council as soon as the bank closes, and . . ."

"My daughter is in jail. One of my men is dead. Another is also in jail. And all you can do is call a meeting?"

"I'm doing the best I can, Hanson. We have a

situation here . . ."

"You sure have. You have had for a long time. . ."

"You hired the man, Hanson."

"It's no use," Friendly told his foreman as they left the bank. "Hell, Fallon's in control. See all the strange gunmen hanging around? We're going to have to do it ourselves. When are the men going to get here?"

"They'll start early in the afternoon. Clayton said he would take over the water tower after they're in place . . ."

"I hope we have enough men," Friendly said.

"I think we will. I think Rocklin's right about that. He's going to be out at the junction?" Friendly nodded. "I guess he'll handle that," Batch said.

"I expect so," the rancher said in a mild tone, and his foreman glanced at him curiously. "I'd better go see Mildred," he said suddenly.

Batch wondered if his boss could talk to the woman without tipping her off that he knew everything. "Do you have to?" he asked.

"I ought to. If I don't, she's bound to wonder why. What a mess."

But they couldn't find Mildred Stocker, or Bracken, or Flack. Ollie Winslow was hard at work at the smithy, however. Batch had convinced Friendly that Winslow could be trusted, and when they stopped to talk, Friendly didn't waste words. "It's going to blow up tonight," he said.

"It sure is," Winslow said. "I know a dozen men who will be around the jail with 12-gauge shotguns. Fallon isn't going to give up, you know."

"I know," Friendly said heavily.

"He killed the Richards girl," Batch said. He knew that Winslow and the Richards family were close. Friendly glanced at him sharply but didn't say anything.

"What? How do you know?"

"We were told by . . . We know," Friendly said.

"But . . . Why don't you say so, man? He'd be hanging within an hour."

"We just found out. And there's no proof."

"Even so. You know this is going to kill Jeb and Nellie Richards. And proof or not . . ."

"Don't forget," Friendly said, "he's holding Arden."

Clayton had no trouble getting up on the tower; he merely climbed up as if he belonged there. When he was halfway up the man on the catwalk that circled the tank looked down and yelled, "Who are you?"

"Billy the Kid. Who do you think I am?" He didn't look up, so the man above couldn't see much more than the top of his hat.

"You can't come up here. Hold it right there!"

Clayton kept climbing. "Jackson sent me. He wants to see you."

"What for? Stop!" But by now the man was

looking into Clayton's gun. He recognized Clayton, and he knew all about him. "You have no business up here," he said.

"It's all right," Clayton told him. "There's going to be some trouble and I'm here to see that the wrong person doesn't get hurt." He reached over and took the man's gun from its holster and stuck it in his own belt. "You can go or stay, whatever suits you."

The man climbed down, and no one in Friendly ever saw him again.

"I can't figure what all the talk is about," Hanson Friendly said. "You people are all the government this town has. You're supposed to be running it. Now everybody heard Jackson here fire Jack Fallon and I want an answer to a simple question: Was Fallon an officer of the law when he grabbed my daughter and killed one of my men or wasn't he?"

"He was not," Mildred Stocker snapped, and Ollie Winslow agreed.

"He was," Andrew J. Flack insisted. "Jackson had no right . . . What about it, Con?"

"I don't know. I wasn't there," Con Bracken said.

"Well, you've heard the whole thing ten times. Don't you have any opinion at all?" Flack said in a nasty tone. "What about you, Willis?"

"Does it really matter?" the banker asked.

The babble drowned out the possibility of anyone's being heard. Friendly glanced at Batch with an expression of disgust. Jackson sat and looked at his hands in his lap.

Friendly tried a Rocklin tactic. He yelled, "Shut up!" It quieted them momentarily. "Brandon is right about one thing. It doesn't matter a damn. The question is how do I get my daughter out of that jail? There's a fine for carrying a gun in town; that's part of the law. All right, I'll pay the fine. And whatever else she's charged with, it's up to you people to set the bail. That's also law, and there's no one else to do it. Whether Fallon acted officially or not, I want to know, right now, how to get my daughter released."

He lowered his voice. "Now, I don't want outside interference in this town any more than you people do, but if I have to, I'll wire the capital. I still have some friends there. What's it going to be?" Silence; a full minute. "Mildred?" No answer. "Brandon?" No answer. "What about it, Ollie?"

Ollie Winslow came out with it. "We can't get your daughter released right this minute. Fallon has taken over the jail with some of his men and refuses to budge."

Friendly nodded. "At least you've admitted it." His voice was grave. "And you all know that if he takes a notion to kill her he's mean enough to do it. All right, that's it. You people are out of it. I'm going to have to do it my way."

"And ride roughshod over the peace and safety

of the community?" Flack demanded. "You will not. Nobody can take the law into his own hands."

Friendly could only stare at him. "Then deputize me and my men," he told the council.

"A legal mob . . ." Flack began.

"Be quiet, Flack," Mildred Stocker ordered. "It's an idea." Friendly and Batch exchanged glances. They were not fools; they were aware of a possible trap. "But first," she went on, "we should give Jackson one more chance to talk some sense into Fallon's head." Everyone looked at Jackson. It was plain he didn't want to, but he was on the spot. Mildred drove her point home by asking Friendly, "Is that all right with you, Hanson?"

"Whatever works."

Jackson left and there was silence broken occasionally by desultory talk for over half an hour. Then there were two shots. They sat and looked at each other. Friendly and Batch got up and started for the door.

"I'll go with you," Ollie Winslow said.

They found a crowd milling around the town square and several deputies standing around Jackson's body. The marshal's office and jail were wide open, and there was nobody inside.

CHAPTER 23

"They say Jackson was just standing there arguing with Fallon," Winslow reported, "when Fallon drew and shot him twice in the chest. He didn't even care who saw it. The door to the office was wide open and Fallon was sitting with his feet up on the desk. All of a sudden he jumped up and killed Jackson."

"And he still has my daughter," Friendly said.

"That's not the worst of it," Ollie said. "He and six or eight of his men have taken over Grange Hall. You all know what that means."

"It means we'll have to surround the place with anyone who can shoot a gun and blast it to pieces," Mildred said.

"That's what I meant," Ollie explained. "There's plenty of room there, it's two stories and it's a soddie. Do you realize that? It's two feet thick at the bottom and almost a foot at the top. You'd have to have cannon."

"Before we do anything, we need a new marshal," Mildred said. "I say Hanson."

"No. Absolutely not," Flack shouted. "He's directly involved. He doesn't even live in town."

"Flack," Friendly said, "if you open your face once more I'll knock it off." He looked around. "You people have got to know by now that my daughter's life is at stake. I won't stop at anything. And I've had enough of this."

"He has a point, Hanson," Willis said. "But we'll see that you're deputized. What about it, Ollie? Are you willing?"

"I'm willing to try," Ollie said. "Just for now. But I'm no good with a gun. I've never had charge of a single man. What about Randy?"

"No," Flack said, "he's just as—" Friendly's look stopped him.

"He's known and liked by everyone," Ollie argued. "He's lived in town all his life, and you might say he still lives here. His folks are here. And after what Fallon tried to do to him . . . well, the whole town will be on his side."

Friendly looked at his foreman. "You don't have to do it, son."

"Try to stop me," Batch said.

The people in the room were aware of a growing clamor outside. Word of the killing had gotten around; a crowd had gathered and it was getting ugly.

"I want it unanimous and on the record," Friendly snapped, looking at Flack. Flack hesitated, then said, "It's unanimous."

"Fallon's gunslingers seem to be gone," Batch

remarked as he and Friendly and Ollie walked toward Grange Hall.

"Yes," Friendly said. "I guess the men at the junction are in for it. I've got one suggestion, son."

The foreman knew there would be more, but he was just as glad. "You're the boss."

"No, you are. But I'd get half a dozen men with shotguns and have them disarm every deputy they see. We don't need anyone at our backs." Friendly was calm now; he was used to calculating and facing odds. Ollie said he would pick the men and Batch told him to go ahead. Two Double H riders fell into step and Randy Batcheler asked them if the snipers were in place. He was told that they had to move when Fallon moved, and one was now in the livery stable loft because there was a back door to Grange Hall. Batch looked around at windows and roofs, and four of his men saw the look and showed themselves at once. They were wide awake and ready.

Batch stopped in the street where everyone could see him and pinned on a badge Brandon Willis had given him. "Just so there'll be no misunderstanding," he told Friendly. Part of the crowd cheered. There was shouting and some applause.

"He caught us with our pants down," one of the cowhands told Batch. "He moved too sudden." He glanced at Friendly. "And he was using Miss Friendly as a shield."

"Is Clayton on the tower?" Friendly asked.

"I saw him go up and I haven't seen him come

down. I don't see what good it is, though, since Fallon moved. Look at his line of sight."

Clayton had long since decided the same thing; he just didn't want to leave the tower until he saw how things were developing. He had been there two hours and it was almost dark. He climbed down and joined the men who were collecting guns from the remaining deputies. The lawmen gave them up without a word. Only one man thought he would make an issue of it, but when he saw six shotguns pointed at his head and heard them being cocked he thought better of it.

Batch had his men all around Grange Hall, except for a narrow strip of ground between the hall and the jail. The hall was a corner building and on a lot of its own, set well back from the main street and the side street with grass all around. There were forty guns pointed at the building, and only two ways out.

Batch, Friendly, Ollie, and Clayton picked a spot next to a tree in the square, directly across from the front entrance to the hall. "Fallon!" Batch shouted. "You might as well give it up. You're not going anywhere." No sound from the hall. "We can stay here until you starve, you know." A wild volley from the four windows of the hall, two upper and two lower. A couple of the onlookers in the square were nicked and the crowd scattered like chickens under attack by hawks.

"Fallon!" Batch called. "What do you expect to get out of this? You're through in this town, but you could ride out. Have some sense. Call it off before you kill someone else." He was answered by a few shots, then it was quiet again.

"What about you other men in there? You're in the clear so far. Can't you see that Fallon isn't going to be able to deliver on anything he's promised you? Give it up. Do you hear me? If anything happens to those two prisoners you're all dead men. Give it up while you still can."

The door to the hall opened slightly and a voice called, "All right. Hold your fire. We're coming out." There were two shotgun blasts from the building and two men stumbled into the street and pitched forward, dead. The door slammed and there was another wild volley from the windows.

"So much for that," Friendly said. "It's hopeless now."

"We'll keep talking," Batch said.

CHAPTER 24

Rocklin and twenty men from the Double H reached Alice Junction about sundown and started to work. The day before, Rocklin had noticed two large stacks of old ties that had been replaced with new ones. The plan was to build four crude redoubts, two on each side of the trail leading into the junction and about a quarter of a mile away. Rocklin was sure Fallon's men would come that way; night riders usually kept to the trails.

When the job was almost finished and night had settled in, U.S. Marshal Ray Cleary rode in from the opposite direction with twenty more men.

"We came down the railroad from Gridley," he explained, "cut south a couple of miles east of here, and circled back. No use trampling over yesterday's tracks too much on the Gridley trail. Somebody might notice and smell trouble. I'm Ray Cleary."

"Just in time, Marshal," Rocklin said. "These are Hanson Friendly's men. My name is Rocklin."

The work was quickly finished. Rocklin had the men roll a drum of kerosene a hundred yards farther down the trail, gouge out a shallow ditch across the trail, set the drum off to the side, and punch a couple of holes at the bottom of it. It would leak for some time. He told one of Friendly's men, "Stay here. Out of sight. When the raiders are past this point toss a match and scoot."

The tent people were crowded into one of the far redoubts and the children were taken to stay overnight with the families in the soddies where they would be safe from wild shots.

"Rocklin, huh?" the marshal said as the two watched men took positions. "You're the man who kills gunmen who are laying for him with a knife."

"It gets wilder with the telling," Rocklin said. "You know that."

"Sure." It was more like "shore" in the marshal's drawl. "But the thing is, I've been a lawman for twenty-five years, I mean all over the West, and the past few years I've heard tall stories and rumors here and there about a special kind of trouble-shooter. Once or twice I've heard a name that sounded something like yours."

Rocklin didn't reply at once. It took some thinking over. A man didn't repeat gossip about a stranger to the stranger's face. Usually, privacy was respected. The marshal had a reason.

The marshal easily read Rocklin's hesitation and added, "Thought you might like to know."

"Thanks," Rocklin said. It took some thinking over, all right, but there wasn't much time for it. Fallon's raiders were coming down the trail.

It was a turkey shoot. The riders were well into the trap when there was a loud whoof and flames lit the sky behind them. Most of the men wondered what was happening; a few realized right away that the trap had closed and it was all over. Some threw their guns down and their hands up without firing a shot; others, more desperate, wanted men, fought savagely and died; two or three took a chance on the dark prairie and escaped south or east.

One man, a dynamiter, had brought up the rear at some distance because too many men didn't want to be anywhere near him. The plan had been to blow up the railroad tracks about every hundred yards for half a mile to discourage any thought of rebuilding. When the "whoof" came, the dynamiter was almost on top of it, and he lost no time turning his horse around and heading back the way he came. But a stray bullet from a Winchester hit a saddlebag. There was a spectacular explosion that would have been heard in Friendly, twenty miles away, if the wind had been right, and then nothing but a large hole in the ground.

The great Alice Junction raid was over. Half of the Double H men got busy right away controlling several spotty grass fires and the rest helped round up the dazed outlaws.

Rocklin asked Marshal Cleary if he was needed and was told he wasn't. He told Friendly's ramrod that he had business in town and headed west. Buck was jumpy after the blast and welcomed a chance to stretch out. Behind them, six men were dead, twelve were headed into Gridley with their hands tied behind them, and two or three were missing. Not one of Friendly's men or a member of the posse had a scratch.

CHAPTER 25

Someone had spaced kerosene torches around Grange Hall. The men inside had tried to stop the operation, but the thick walls had a drawback. Windowsills were set far into the walls and a man had to stick his head out to get a good shot at someone who approached close to the side of the building. After a couple of the men inside just about had their heads shot off, the torches stayed.

Rocklin took Buck to the livery stable and asked the man if he would rub him down before he watered and fed him. "He's hot and tired."

"I'll take care of him," the man assured Rocklin, and then filled him in on what had been happening. Rocklin circled the small downtown and walked to the square.

Hanson Friendly said, "What are you doing here? What happened?"

Rocklin described the scene at Alice Junction, but Friendly showed no satisfaction. "You've won, Mr. Friendly. This is the end of it."

"I haven't won anything if something happens to my daughter."

"What's been done?" Rocklin asked.

"Batch here is in charge. He's the marshal, temporarily."

"Not much," Batch volunteered. "Every time I tell him he hasn't got a chance and he ought to give it up, they throw a few more shots and that's it. We're saving our ammunition. I figure waiting is worse for him than it is for us."

Clayton walked up and said, "Hi, Rocklin. How did it go?"

"Shooting fish in a barrel. Fallon's alone now, except for the men in there with him. How many are there?"

"Six at most; maybe only four or five," Batch said. "He killed two of them who tried to give up. Buckshot in the back."

"They got ropes to the roof," Clayton told Batch. "There's a man on top already. It's solid. The only openings are the chimneys."

Batch explained to Rocklin: "There are only four small windows in the back and they're high up in the inside wall. It's a blind spot for Fallon, and we can put a dozen men on the roof."

"What for?" Friendly asked.

"I don't know," Batch admitted. "I just want them there. How big are the chimneys?" he asked Clayton. "Did you get an idea?"

"The front ones are big enough for a skinny

192

man to get down. But it would be suicide. We couldn't cover the sound no matter how much noise we made out here; the walls are too thick. They might be useful as a diversion."

Batch nodded. "If worse comes to worst," he told Rocklin, "we'll have to go in. We can get men right up to both doors. The back one is easy. The front will be a little harder but it can be done. A man can approach from the back and Indian-crawl around the building, and if he's careful enough he won't be seen from those windows; they're set too far back in the wall, see? A man can get right up next to the front door. We'll put three or four at the front and as many as we can get at the back. At a signal, they'll blast the locks with a shotgun and all go in at once. We'll unload everything we've got at the windows," he smiled grimly, "and maybe even down the chimneys, just before we go in. Fallon will be too rattled to bother with . . ." the marshal swallowed hard ". . . with the girl. Clayton and I will go in at the front . . ."

"I'll go in the back," Rocklin said.

"We'll go in together," Friendly said.

Batch nodded. "We probably ought to have three or four more volunteers . . ."

"I'm going in," Ollie Winslow said.

"So am I," a tall, bony man in denim jacket and coveralls said.

They all looked at him. Ollie said, "This is Jeb Richards." They nodded and the bony man was

193

part of the group.

"So are we." Two young men stepped forward hesitantly. They were dressed alike and impossible to tell apart. Around town they were called the Missouri twins.

"Who are you?" Batch asked.

"Our name is Jacobs," one of them said. "Bill and Bob Jacobs from Joplin."

"A couple of Jackson's deputies," Ollie Winslow said.

"Give us a chance, Mr. Batcheler," the other brother urged. "We won't let you down. We give you our word. We've worn badges in a *real* town." They stood quietly while Batch looked into their faces.

"Take 'em to the jail, will you, Ollie, and let them pick out their guns. Give them their badges." Nobody disagreed.

"But it is a last resort," Batch said. "We'll outwait them if we can. What about it, Mr. Rocklin?"

Rocklin was nodding slowly. "Maybe, in the meantime, we ought to think of as many ways as we can to get on their nerves. I have a hunch that if we all drew back, just disappeared for an hour and stayed quiet . . . it would surely set them to wondering.

Friendly said, "The Indians were good at that. It's an idea."

"First let me do something," Clayton said. "Batch, I want to call Fallon out. Is it worth a

194

try?"

"I would say yes" was Batch's immediate reply.

"Go to it," Friendly said.

Clayton stood in plain sight next to the nearest tree across from the hall. "Fallon! Can you hear me, Fallon?"

"I can see you too. I can put one right between your eyes. What's on your mind?"

"I'm wearing a gun, Fallon. This is your chance. Why don't you get out from behind that skirt and come out and die like a man." He glimpsed a flicker of light on a gun barrel and ducked behind the tree as a bullet tore off a piece of bark.

Fallon laughed. "Do you think I'm a fool! I need the skirt. I'll get a chance at you later. I'm coming out of here alive, do you hear me? Do you all hear me? If I don't, I'll blow the girl's face off and shove her out the front door. Would you like to see your girl's face blown off, Friendly?"

"If you do that, we'll hang you so you'll kick for an hour before you die," Clayton said. "Wouldn't you rather come out and kill me and get it over with?"

Fallon laughed and got off another shot.

"Let's make 'em sit and think about it for an hour," Batch said.

The hour seemed like five. A few people, women and children, went home but most would stay until it was over. Talk was the most important pastime in that lonely country, and that night

195

would provide enough talk for a generation.

Fallon was pacing back and forth and his five remaining men were sitting or hunkered down against a wall watching him. Arden and the cowhand with her, named Verlie, were sitting against the opposite wall. Their hands were cuffed behind their backs.

"Why don't you loosen his handcuffs, you beast," Arden said. "His hands are turning blue. If gangrene sets in he'll lose them."

"Shut your mouth, missy, or I'll slap it shut." Verlie got up and charged at Fallon like a bull, with his head down. Fallon chopped at the side of his head with a six-shooter and Verlie hit the floor, unconscious. One of the gunmen came over and looked at Verlie's hands.

"She's right," he said. "He's liable to lose his hands. Why don't you loosen them, Fallon."

Fallon dipped fingers into a vest pocket, tossed a key to the gunman, and said, "Don't take 'em off." He strode to a front window, smashed it with his rifle, and yelled, "What's going on out there?" The answer was silence. He cussed a stream and emptied his rifle, spraying shots at random around the square.

"It's working," Batch said in a low voice. He and the others were sitting behind trees at the far side of the square.

"It sure is," Clayton said. "I hope he doesn't go completely off the rails." Then he glanced at

Friendly.

Friendly was standing, leaning with his back to a tree. His face was impassive. He looked older.

"We'll get her out, Hanson," Clayton said.

Friendly came alert. He was peering through the darkness along the north-south street bordering the far side of the square. Something was coming. It was a buggy. Alice Friendly's buggy. People were standing up, watching. It stopped in front of Friendly and people gathered around. Alice Friendly stepped out. She was wearing boots and a split buckskin skirt and jacket. Her white head was bare. She stood tall and straight, an impressive figure.

Hanson Friendly went to her and gave her his hand. He said, "Alice."

"Are you going to tell me I shouldn't have come, Hanson?"

"No. No, I'm not."

"It had been too long. I knew something was wrong." She wasn't scolding him for not letting her know because she knew he thought he was being more thoughtful than thoughtless.

"I'm glad you came," he assured her.

People were drawing back deferentially. Alice Friendly gave an immediate impression of aloofness, but those who knew her knew she was warm and friendly and unaffected. There was almost no resentment of her in the town. She was saying hello to people and they were answering, Hello,

197

Alice or Hello Mrs. Friendly.

When she and her husband had drawn apart from the crowd she asked, "How bad is it, Hanson?"

He told it straight. "We have the upper hand. But he still has Arden."

"I see. I want to ask him to let her go. Would you object too much?"

"Of course not." He ventured a little lie. "It might do some good."

One of Fallon's men was looking out a front window. "There's some movement out there," he said. The other men went to windows. Arden and Verlie sat still.

When Alice Friendly was in position next to a tree, she called, "Mr. Fallon!"

Arden got up quickly and started toward a window, but one of the men intercepted her and dragged her farther back into the hall.

There was silence for half a minute, then Fallon called, "Who's that?"

"It's Alice Friendly, Mr. Fallon." The "Mr. Fallon" set her husband's teeth on edge but he didn't say anything. "Why don't you let our daughter go, Mr. Fallon. She's everything to us and she's nothing to you."

"If I didn't have her I'd be dead now. Do you understand, lady? It's no use. Go home."

"We're all going to be dead eventually, Mr. Fallon. Give yourself this chance. Let her go."

"Go home, dammit!" He threw a wild shot at the tree.

Batch spoke up. "Fallon! This is Batcheler. We've set up shifts. We can stay here forever if we have to. You other men in there. We saw what happened to the two who tried to give up. We can take it that you're being forced to stay. You're in the clear if you give up now."

Fallon laughed. "They're dead if they give up now. Besides, they took my money and they're with me in this. They're not cowards."

"How is our daughter?" Friendly shouted.

"She's all right so far," Fallon said. "She's a regular little tiger, you know that? I tried to get her to a window so I could make her beg everybody to go away. She said she'd see me in hell first." He laughed. "Your daughter is no lady, Friendly, but she's a fighter. I like that. She'll be fun when I get her where I want her." He laughed again.

Batch took a chance. "Like the Richards girl?" he shouted. He thought it would give Fallon something more to think about.

Fallon didn't answer for a while. Then he said, "Mildred Stocker has been shooting off her mouth, has she? Why don't you get her to come and ask me to give up and see what she says. I'll bet she would blow up this building and everyone in it if she could put the blame on somebody else. You people are stupid, you know that? That old battleaxe has all the money she ever squeezed from this town, every penny. She set the whole thing up, you know. You people are too stupid to live." The laugh came again, this time with a chilling undertone. The man was throwing everything away, burning every bridge.

"It's only a matter of time," Clayton said. "We'd better get ready to go in."

"You're right," Batch said. "We'll take the front with the Jacobs twins." He looked their way. "All right?"

"Right," they said together.

"Mr. Friendly, Rocklin, Ollie, and Richards will take the back. We'll have to pass the word first, no shooting until I say so . . ."

"We'd better get rid of some of the guns around here," Clayton said. "People have been waiting for a long time. They're bound to be edgy. They could fill us full of holes."

"You're right. But it will take awhile to explain it to them. We'd better get everything as straight as we can before we start. I wish they were all home asleep . . ."

"Hanson," Alice Friendly said. Her husband looked at her with respect. "Offer the men inside money."

"What do you mean?"

"Offer them money and freedom if they kill Fallon. Offer them ten thousand dollars."

The astonished men looked at her for just a few

200

seconds. Then they looked at each other. Batch was almost holding his breath. "It might work," he whispered. "What do you think, Mr. Friendly?"

"I'll do it."

"Rocklin? Tom?"

"Try it," Clayton said promptly.

"Yes," Rocklin agreed, then added, "wait a minute, though." A question had been worrying him. What was Fallon waiting for? Whatever his original plan had been, he must know that he blew it to pieces when he lost control of his temper and killed Jackson. If he really planned to take Arden Friendly, why didn't he take her right then and get out, while he had the chance? He had to be stalling for some reason, and that reason was obvious: He was waiting for his gang to get back from Alice Junction. Then if he released Arden at just the right time, Friendly and his people just might take her home and leave him to the town. And the town would be no match for Fallon and his gang. They could sack it and take off.

"Well?" Friendly asked.

"You might tell him that his men aren't coming back from Alice Junction, that he has no men left," Rocklin said.

"Good idea," Batch said.

"Fallon!" Friendly shouted. "I want to talk to one of your men."

"What about? You talk to me. Who do you know in here? What man?"

"I don't know what man. You'll hear me. I'm talking to the man with sense enough and sand enough to walk up behind you and put a bullet in your head. Ten thousand dollars for that man, and he'll walk out free. Listen, you men, you have my word, and nobody can say I ever went back on my word."

Silence. "Fallon. You might as well know that your gang isn't coming to break you out. They're all on their way to territorial prison, the ones that aren't dead. You've got no hole card, Fallon."

There were sounds of movement from the hall, faintly like a scuffle, and three or four gunshots; it was hard to tell, they came so fast. Then silence. It didn't last long.

"Friendly!" Fallon yelled. An audible groan rippled over the square. "They had no brains and no guts. They weren't even men. You lost, Friendly, and now you have just ten minutes to get everybody out of here. Everybody! And I want five horses at the back door. Ten minutes, Friendly, and I blow your snotty daughter's face off."

"He means it," Batch said. "We've got to go in. Now."

"It's better this way," Clayton said. "We can get rid of all the farmers and clerks. Beg pardon, Mr. Richards."

"No offense," the bony man said. "You're right."

They started off.

"Wait," Rocklin said. They stopped. Friendly glanced at him and started to leave anyway. Then he looked at him again.

"What is it, Mr. Rocklin?" Alice Friendly asked.

"This could be what you've all been waiting for. Has anyone seen the girl? All the time you've been here? Heads were shaken. "Then how do you know she's alive?"

"I know," Friendly rasped. "Don't you think I'd know? Besides, what Fallon said is exactly like her. What's the idea of this, Rocklin?"

"Wait, Hanson," Alice Friendly said. "Go on, Mr. Rocklin."

"It's simple. Demand to see her. All of her, alive and well. Not at a window. You can't see anything. At the front door. He's got to open the front door and show her. Otherwise, the next time he threatens to kill her you're going to figure she's already dead and start dropping sticks of dynamite down the chimneys. Can you do it?"

"And Rocklin and Tom and I will be at the front door," Batch said. "And Ollie, you and Richards will be on one side of the building, right at the front," he turned to the Jacobs twins, "and you two men will be on the other side."

"I think . . ." Rocklin began.

"What?" Batch asked.

"Maybe the fewer people bunched around the front of the building the better."

Batch didn't have to consider for two seconds.

"Right. Only two men, then. You and Tom. I have a feeling you're both a lot faster than I am. I'll take the twins, and as soon as I hear shooting in front we'll go in the back."

"Ollie, you and Richards can do the most good by passing the word to everyone in the square that there will be no shooting. No shooting at all, understand? We don't want anyone getting killed for no reason. We'd better go."

"Where are your riflemen?" Rocklin asked Friendly.

"Two on top of the firehouse, right there across the street, and two on top of the jail. They'll be shooting at an angle, but they'll have clear shots, with the hall set back the way it is."

"If you bluff it out, she'll have a lot better chance," Rocklin told the rancher. "It's up to you."

Friendly turned to his wife. "Alice?"

The woman's eyes were closed and her head was slightly bowed. She was as still as a stone. Then she looked at her husband. "Either way," she said, "her chances don't appear too good, do they? If she's going to die, I would like to see her one more time."

The men moved off quickly. "All right," Batch shouted, "you all heard him. Clear the square. Hurry. Somebody, you, Bracken, and you, Willis, go over to the stable and get five horses. We haven't got much time."

"Five minutes, Friendly," Fallon shouted.

"We're bringing the horses, Fallon," Friendly shouted back. "You'll just have to wait until they get here. But how do I know my daughter is even alive? I want to see her."

"Four minutes," Fallon shouted.

"Get it straight, Fallon. The streets and square are being cleared, and you'll get your horses. But I'm not doing this for a dead girl. Either I see her standing in the front door, alive and unhurt in four minutes or we start dropping dynamite down the chimneys." There was no answer from the hall. "Make up your mind, Fallon. All I want is to make sure my daughter is alive and you've got an open road out of here. You know I'd be a fool to take your word for it. Let me see her, Fallon."

"Get the men off the roof," Fallon yelled.

"No. They're going to start dynamiting in three minutes. Show her, Fallon. You've got nothing to lose and everything to gain by just letting us see her."

"She's at the window with me now." He was twisting her arm, trying to make her cry out so they could hear her, but she wouldn't make a sound. She started to faint with the pain and he let up. Verlie was struggling with two gunmen in a vain effort to get to her.

"We can't see anything through the window. You ought to know that. At the door, Fallon."

The men were in place.

"Two minutes, Fallon. You know I'm not going

to kill my own daughter if I know she's alive. But I've got to know."

There was dead silence for another minute, then the door of the hall started to creak open.

"All right, take a look at her," Fallon yelled.

"You know I can't see her. You're lying, Fallon. You've killed her already."

"What's the matter with you? Look at her. Can't you see her now?"

Arden was almost all the way out the door. Fallon had her pinned around the waist and was holding a shotgun to her right temple. She saw Clayton pressed against the wall within inches of her to the right. She didn't let on. She couldn't see Rocklin on the other side of the door but she knew someone was there.

"All right, that's enough. You've seen her," Fallon yelled.

Arden went suddenly limp in his arm. At the same time she stepped hard on his injured foot. The cracked bones gave way and Fallon half fell out of the doorway, jamming the shotgun muzzle into the ground to catch himself.

Clayton had his gun at the back of Fallon's head in a split second, with the hammer cocked. Fallon was using his shotgun as a crutch and his Colt was in his holster. Clayton hesitated, not wanting to splash the man's brains on Arden. A bullet creased his wrist and nicked the bone. His gun jumped sideways and in reflex he pulled the trigger, blowing Fallon's ear off. It happened too fast for thought.

Two more bullets screamed in, one hitting the front of the building and the other going through the open door. Rocklin jerked the door all the way open, grabbed Arden and threw her to the ground, piling on top of her just as he felt something hot tug at his ribs next to his heart. Fallon used his shotgun as a lever to propel himself over Rocklin and the girl. Clayton was pointing his gun, but for a second there was just a tangle of bodies to shoot at. Then Fallon rose in a crouch and hurled himself at the corner of the building.

Five men, Clayton and four snipers, now had fairly clear shots at him. Four shots hit him as, half hopping and half running, he rounded the corner and was gone.

The shooting stopped—the men knew Fallon was dead, anyway—and Rocklin rolled off Arden, feeling his side to see how bad it was. It was not serious, but it would need some attention later. "Take care of her," he told Clayton, and followed Fallon down between the hall and the jail.

When Batch and his men blasted the back door open and went through, they found Verlie leaning against a wall and three gunmen stretching their arms as high as they could go. Batch ran on through the hall to see if Arden was all right and helped Clayton half lead and half carry her across the street.

She was sick with remorse and could hardly speak above a whisper. "I'm so sorry, Daddy. I'm so sorry." Friendly patted her heavily on the shoulder. "What am I going to do, Mother? Dan Racey is dead because of me. And Verlie . . . he attacked Fallon with his hands shackled. What am I going to do?" She went to Clayton. "I'm so sorry, Tom." She turned to Batch. "Can you ever forgive me, Randy? Oh, Randy!" She threw her arms around his neck and the tears came. Batch was nearly paralyzed. He kept patting her gingerly on the back and saying, "It's all right, Ardie. It's all over."

Rocklin walked toward the back of the hall, following Fallon. There was no hurry. The man was staggering. He managed to reach the back corner and head for the horses standing a few yards away.

He stopped dead and stared at Mildred Stocker, not three paces in front of him. She had a shotgun and was pointing it at him. He tried to go for his six-shooter. She fired both barrels, almost cutting him in two.

Rocklin stopped in the shadow of the hall and watched Mildred Stocker. She had a crutch and was holding it tight to her side with the upper part of an arm and an elbow as she traveled fast over the ground toward her store. At the same time, she was using her hands to reload the shotgun. People were in the way, running toward the square from the livery stable and some of the houses beyond. Rocklin dodged them, trying not to lose sight of Mildred. He thought there was some reason to hurry and started to run. She was headed for the storage shed in back of her store. She was pointing the shotgun at the shed.

A picture flashed through Rocklin's mind of the town where he was standing being smashed by a hellish explosion of fire. He drew his gun and shot Mildred between the shoulder blades. In the same instant he heard a rifle bark up ahead and to his right.

Mildred Stocker went to her knees, but she raised the shotgun again and pointed it at the dynamite-filled shed. Rocklin shot her again. This time he saw the muzzle flash from the rifle. It was being fired by Newton Stocker. His wife was lying face down in the dirt, her gun and her crutch lying beside her.

Newton Stocker walked over and put a bullet in the back of her head.

CHAPTER 26

There was only the faintest touch of light in the east when Rocklin fetched Buck from the stable and headed out of town. The wind that had talked in strange voices all night around the doors and windows of the hotel had slacked off some, but it was already warm. He was glad to be seeing the last of the town called Friendly.

He avoided the main street and the square and had just connected with the trail north when he heard a light wagon, or a buggy, coming up behind him. He pulled up and turned. It was Alice and Hanson Friendly, on their way home after a few hours' sleep at the hotel.

"They said you had left, Mr. Rocklin," Alice Friendly said. "And we were concerned about you. Tom Clayton said you had been wounded."

"Very slightly, ma'am. The doctor patched me up in no time at all."

"You are coming out for a few days, aren't you? We haven't had a chance to express our thanks."

"You just did," Rocklin assured her. "And I'm supposed to be in Kansas City right now, and I still have a couple of people to see in the east county."

"Look, Rocklin," Friendly growled, "I'm more than just obliged to you. You pulled it off and I still can't believe it. I would have made a total mess of it. Then . . . well, I saw how you protected Arden last night . . ."

"I was just there. Any man . . ."

"No. Not just any man. I'm in your debt. More than I can ever pay."

"You *can* do something," Rocklin said.

"Name it."

Rocklin laughed shortly. "Never mention my name again." Alice Friendly knew immediately what he meant, but Hanson was for a moment taken aback. "There are plenty of people to talk about," Rocklin said.

Friendly was nodding. "And you're just a cattle buyer who happened to get caught in between."

"That's true enough. And all deals are still good. That's why I'm going to Kansas City. Shafter's main offices are there."

"And that's it?"

"That's it," Rocklin assured him.

"You know," Friendly said, "Newton's talking already. First time anyone in this town ever heard him. I don't know if you know about it or not, but we found two large Gladstone bags stuffed

211

with money in that shed."

"Is that a fact?"

"Looks like it could be as much as two hundred thousand dollars. Willis took it to the bank and it's going to be counted this morning. They were sitting there on a neat stack of her records, all of her records. She actually planned to blow up the whole town if she couldn't hang on to it."

"What did Newton have to say?"

"That it was just like her. Said he wanted no part of the money. There was talk by a couple of councilmen last night of giving it back; using Mildred's records, I mean. Looks like the biggest chunk of it belongs to me."

"And will you take it?" Rocklin asked.

Alice Friendly smiled and Hanson laughed drily. "You're a calculating man, Rocklin, and you don't miss a thing, do you? I don't know. Not all of it, that's sure. But real generosity is not remembered for very long, is it? A man might just as well be quiet about it. But if you can do something that's mostly ballyhoo . . ." He laughed again. "Well, leave that to the politicians.

"Anyway, it's not my town now."

For two days in a row, Arden Friendly got up before dawn and vanished into the prairie until nightfall while Tom Clayton waited for her to approach him.

212

When she did, in midmorning of the third day, he said, "Feeling better?"

"No," she said, "I'm feeling worse. But I'm thinking better, I hope. Why are you still here? Why are you bothering with me? How's your wrist?"

Clayton had started into town, and when he had heard a horse behind him had turned and waited for her. "I'm fine," he said.

She invited him to dismount and walk with her by dismounting herself. He thought it would be much less awkward if they were afoot when he kissed her and decided that was why she did it. He was right.

She clung to him for what he thought was a long time, and he eased the pressure of his arms to invite her to end it if she wanted to. "No. Not yet," she said. She was feeling the strength of his chest and shoulders and arms, and the turmoil in her mind and heart was smoothing out. She didn't feel like kissing him again; she felt . . . quieter. Finally she gently withdrew and said, rather primly, "Thank you."

He laughed at her softly and said, "You're welcome."

When they had mounted again she asked, "Where were you going?"

"Into town. I thought I'd see how Batch is doing."

"Oh yes, let's," she said.

213

They rode in silence, until he asked, "How is the mental war going? Any armistice yet?"

"Yes. And you know, it's like I imagine lots of wars to be. When it's over you wonder what it was all about. All that carnage over such an insignificant prize. My mind, I mean."

The animated expression he found so appealing vanished for an instant and there was genuine pain there. He tried to think of something to say that wouldn't sound stupid; there wasn't anything. He reached over and patted her shoulder. The gratitude in her glance was genuine too.

"I'm sorry," she said. "I'm finding out how much a person can actually dislike herself without dying."

"You're not going off the deep end in the other direction, are you?"

She gave the question serious thought. It was, he decided, one of her most endearing traits. "No," she said.

It sounded like the answer to any question he might ask.

The next day when Clayton was taking his leave, saying good-bye all around, he pulled up at the patio where Arden was standing. "You will come, won't you?" he urged. "Bring your family. Spend the winter." He looked at her mother. "We have mild winters in my corner of the country, Mrs. Friendly. Won't you come?"

"You just tell us when," Alice Friendly said.

He bent down, swept Arden up with one arm and kissed her. Her face was flushed and she laughed a bit breathlessly when he set her down. "I thought for a moment you were going to throw me across your saddle," she said. He took a long look at her face and rode away.

CHAPTER 27

Mary Tillman
17 Washington Square Place
New York City, New York

My beloved wife,
Just a note, which, I hope, finds you and the children well.

I am heading home. I am sitting in a rickety hotel in the little town of Gridley in Dakota Territory and in about three hours I will catch a train going east. I must stop in Kansas City and Chicago, so I will be home a few days, maybe a week, after you receive this.

I was wondering if we might take a year or so and go on a trip around the world. It could be arranged. We could take a tutor along for young Bill and little Louise. We wouldn't have to go on one of my ships if you wanted to avoid a captain who is oversolicitous. We could take an English ship, one of the new White Star steamers. They go wherever there is a British colony, which means all over the world.

I know that I have already suggested winter at the ranch, so you will no doubt guess that I am not in the most cheerful frame of mind. Now, don't concern yourself. There is nothing really wrong. It's just that this latest business has left me wondering about the point of it all.

An entire town trusted a group of men to impose perfect order, and I am wondering if what it ended up with is better or worse than no order at all.

I am wondering too whether the town called Friendly will now drift toward the opposite extreme. I suppose the contradictory nature of the human creature means that we will never be able to resolve such dilemmas. Meanwhile, whatever the extreme, the predators will try to step in and take over. But enough.

Something you said before I left indicated to me that you have an idea why I go on jobs like this. You told me to take care and then added that the man I'm looking for might long since be dead. You are right, as usual, but I'm not really looking for the man who murdered Bobby. Twelve years is too long a time, too long to hate.

I have had some experience with hate, as you know, and it burns life out of everything, like a hot prairie wind. And my love for you and the children is very much alive. There, do you see? All I know beyond that is that there are some very bad men in the world who are very hard to stop.

Somehow I find all this (nonsense, probably) easier to write than to say.

You are most precious to me.

Your husband,

William R. Tillman

CHAPTER 28

"You're lucky she didn't get you with that shot-gun."

Rocklin and Tom Clayton were sitting in a small restaurant across from Kansas City's Union Station finishing off steak dinners and drinking coffee. They had met unexpectedly about an hour before while waiting for trains, Rocklin for his to Chicago and Clayton for his to Dallas via Missouri, Kansas, and Oklahoma.

"It was very close," Rocklin said. "I could almost feel it. She would have too, right there in the office, but she suspected, rightly, that it was too late for that. So she took one last chance and offered the bribe."

"Whatever made you think of her in the first place?"

"A combination of things. The first day, she spoke up and Fallon backed off, remember? And it seemed to me she was the most accessible, to Fallon, I mean, if he was reasonably careful.

219

"Then there was Fallon's unofficial office. I always had the feeling we were being overheard.

"But finally it was just elimination. When I had crossed everyone else off, she was left. It wasn't all that hard; there weren't very many possibilities."

"Did you find out who sent me the letter?"

"I figure it could only have been Newton. Fallon was the only one in town who knew who you were, it seemed to me. So Mildred also knew. And Newton . . . well, Newton never spoke. A man who never speaks can hear a lot. Besides, he warned me about Gasser Mann."

Clayton had always assumed that Rocklin had killed Gasser. He wasn't curious about that. But he was curious about something else, something he was hesitant to bring up. But finally he did.

"When you suggested that Friendly tell Fallon he had no men left, I thought Arden was a goner."

"You're right. She was. She was his only way out, then. He'd have to take her along for protection. But he was going to realize that anyway when his men didn't show up."

Clayton didn't know what to say. He realized for the first time just how ruthless a man had to be in Rocklin's line of work.

"An unusual girl," he said. "Although I don't know why I call her a girl."

"Very unusual."

"I wouldn't be surprised if Friendly finds himself a son soon, right there on his own ranch," Clayton ventured.

"Neither would I," Rocklin said. "Have you been to New York?"

Clayton abandoned the subject of Arden Friendly with a certain relief. "A few times. It's quite a town. Do you actually have electric street lighting now?"

"Spreading like a prairie fire. We don't have electric streetcars yet—we're a little behind Richmond and Baltimore there—but we will. You'll have to stay with us the next time you're there."

"Us?" Clayton asked.

"I have a wife and two children."

"I will be damned."

Rocklin wrote on a piece of paper and handed it to Clayton. "My name and address. The little number is what you ask Central for to get me on the telephone." He laughed. "And now that you know all about me, forget you know me."

Clayton was eyeing him. "You don't completely trust anyone, do you?"

"I didn't mean that the way it sounded, Tom. I meant if you ever run across me out West. It goes with the job. When too many people know about me I'll have to quit. The people who pay me will know the odds are turning against me and they'll write me off."

"Obvious," Clayton said. "I should have known." He was thoughtful, nodding to himself. "New Mexico. You told me you had a ranch there. I know a couple of ranchers . . . that trouble in Sweetwater . . ."

"It's a matter of avoiding complications," Rocklin said. "Suppose you ran into me down along the Pecos somewhere. You know the country, you get around, so you'd probably guess right away why I was there. And it might be better if you pretended you didn't. I might not even want you to recognize me. Complicaitons,"

"It was a foolish remark," Clayton said. "Forget I made it."

THE SURVIVALIST SERIES
by Jerry Ahern